COMES THE PHOENIX

Stephen Schmidt

Copyright © 2015 Stephen W. Schmidt
All Rights Reserved

No part of this book may be reproduced or transmitted in any form or by any means electronic or mechanical, including photocopying, recording, or by any information storage and retrieval system, without permission in writing by the author.
This is a work of fiction. Names, characters, places, events, or incidents are the product of the author's imagination or are used fictitiously. Any resemblance to actual persons, living or dead, business establishments, events, or locales is purely coincidental.

ISBN: 1514124661
ISBN 13: 9781514124666

Cover Design: Wendy Mersman, Moon Designs, LLC
www.MoonDesigns.com

For C.M.

"And the time came when it was more painful to remain in the bud than it was to risk blossoming."

Anais Nin

"Your soul and my soul once sat together in the Beloved's womb, playing footsie. Your soul and my soul are very old friends."

Hafiz

CHAPTER ONE

Friday evening, finally. It had been a long week and an even longer summer. Sophie would open up the shop in the morning, and it would probably be a relatively easy day at Tyler's Floral & Gifts. Tyler walked a couple of miles along the beach of Lake Michigan. He walked and walked and walked. It seemed as if time was standing still. Somehow, it seemed a much further walk than it actually was from where he had parked his car in the lot to his space of solace. *Why was that?* Tyler wondered as he ran his fingers through his short, sandy brown hair.

He saw the log snuggled in the beach grass and made his way towards it. He chose this spot to rest, sit, ponder, meditate, and make sense of things. Tyler sat his five-foot ten-inch frame down on the log. He noticed dusk was approaching rapidly. Tonight was the New Moon, which would become September's Harvest Moon. A New Moon was always a time when a powerful energy portal would be opened. It would be a time for receiving healing and guidance. Would Mother Moon shine down upon him and allow the answers and peace he sought to flow to him? *I'm ready,* thought Tyler.

Five months ago, Christopher was driving home from Tyler's late at night in a heavy rainstorm. Christopher was an excellent driver, but then out of nowhere, a young drunk driver appeared to be swerving all over the road. In an attempt to avoid hitting him, Christopher's car left the road and rolled over several times before being stopped by a huge oak tree at the bottom of a ravine. That tragic event ended the only loving relationship Tyler had ever known. And that was that. Those who knew Christopher agreed that it was the one and only time in Christopher's life that he was at the wrong place at the wrong time.

Yes, tonight was the evening of a New Moon. New Moons had figured predominantly into Tyler's and Christopher's journey together. It had been a New Moon the evening of Carmella's party, which is where Tyler saw Christopher for the first time. The evening of their first date together had been a New Moon as had been the first time they slept together. *Why was it when two people have sex it is referred to as "sleeping together?"* Tyler smiled recalling there was very little sleeping occurring that particular evening. Once again, the New Moon this evening would figure eminently in Tyler's life. Aware of this, he gratefully welcomed the fact.

Tyler knew all too well that life wasn't fair. He'd had enough lessons in his twenty-eight years to learn that harsh reality. His coming to know and to love Christopher, only to have him taken away so quickly, so very unnecessarily, challenged Tyler to the core. On this evening, Tyler just *knew* that he was prepared to finally understand what he needed to know to move on. He had always found solace in meditating here on the western shore of Lake Michigan. He would stay all night if necessary to listen to what Spirit would tell him.

Tyler noticed three young people, probably in their late teens, walking carefree along the water's edge. In the center, a handsome young man flanked by a young woman on each side appeared laughing with no cares in the world, arm in arm. Tyler wished he was brave enough to run up to them and say, *Enjoy every minute you have together. Cherish them. Savor them, for people are only in your life but a fleeting moment.* Tyler mused, *What's the worst thing that could happen if I did do that? That they might think that I was crazy?* He'd been called worse. The fact that some people thought him odd for his belief system never really bothered him.

Think of all of the people who have been in your life, Tyler. Each one is like a fragment of a broken mirror, a few large shards of glass, and many miniature ones who all were a part of a now-broken life. With a new confidence Tyler spoke to the Universe. "I want to put the pieces back together. I want to see what was there for me once and to take a good long, hard look at what is there for me now. Why did people leave me so soon, each taking a piece with him or her? I need to know, Spirit. And I need to know now, please and thank you."

Tyler's gaze went back to the trio as they sauntered along the beach until they were out of sight. He looked up at the moon as She was beginning to make her presence known, and closed his eyes, drinking in the silence about him. And then they were there. His trinity: Sophie, Tyler, and Magda, arm in arm walking along the same beach at sunset. Dear Magda, his and Sophie's beloved friend and spiritual teacher. The three of them suddenly stopped and faced the setting sun. Following Magda's cue, with arms outstretched embracing the rays of the setting sun. "Thank you for your Love, Light, and Warmth, our dear Sun," Magda spoke.

"There is nothing quite as beautiful as a sunset over the lake. Thank you for this moment," Tyler observed.

"Amen," added Sophie.

There are occasions in life when you meet someone, you feel an instant connection. Sometimes, it's as if you have known them before, and the big plus was they totally accepted you and understood you. That's how it was with Sophie and Magda.

Tyler met Sophie three years ago, the day he opened up his shop, Tyler's Floral and Gifts. She entered the store, asking if he was taking applications. Sophie had been in town a year and had experience in the floral business. The interview, which was really a conversation, lasted an hour. Sophie started work the next day. Although he was a novice student in metaphysics, Tyler understood energy, and he liked Sophie's. He trusted his gut instinct and knew that she would be the perfect assistant for him.

A couple of weeks later, Sophie invited Tyler to go hear her teacher and spiritual advisor, Magda, speak at the public library on reincarnation. Tyler had always been intrigued with the subject although other than reading Shirley MacLaine's books, he hadn't explored the topic to any great depth. Magda Olson was a petite dynamo of energy. Her piercing blue eyes radiated such joy. Her gray hair was neatly secured in a bun. Laugh lines, not wrinkles, graced her tan face. Magda possessed a wealth of metaphysical and spiritual information and shared it willingly with warmth, joy, and sensitivity. Soon thereafter, he started taking classes from her, grateful for her knowledge. In addition to Magda becoming Tyler's teacher, they became fast friends.

In the grand scheme of things, reincarnation was really the only thing that made any sense. If you didn't learn a lesson the first time, then you would be given another opportunity, or lifetime(s) to get it right. Too bad the church had taken so many references to reincarnation out of the Bible in an attempt to control the masses.

And now, as if it were yesterday, Tyler saw himself, Magda and Sophie walking up the long winding driveway of the Kellor estate headed to Carmella's annual benefit extravaganza. Each summer, Carmella Kellor hosted a benefit for one of her favorite charities. This year it was for Emily's House, a shelter for children and their parent(s) who had fallen on hard times. Carmella knew how to entertain and raise money for the causes she believed in. This year's theme was the Roaring Twenties, and guests were to come dressed for that era. The one-hundred-dollar ticket got one admission to the party and plenty of hors d'oeuvres. Everything else, games of chance, a well-stocked bar, the dance competition, all cost money. And people willingly donated. It was always an incredibly fun party that raised thousands. Several hundred attended annually. Tonight, Sophie, Magda, and Tyler planned on entering and winning the Charleston competition and they dressed accordingly. They loved costume parties! Magda chose a black flapper's dress. The black ostrich feather accented her gray hair perfectly. Sophie was in a red fringe flapper's dress, and Tyler was attired in a black suit of the era, complete with a black fedora and cane.

Carmella greeted them at the door. The buxom hostess was wearing a silver flapper's dress. "Welcome to my humble abode!" she belted out. "Look at the three of you! I'm going to have to add a couple of prizes for best costume tonight."

"Wait until after the Charleston competition to see how good anyone still looks," Sophie said. "It might make the judging a little easier," she added as she perused the crowd attired in zoot suits, mobster clothes, Great Gatsby attire, and fringe dresses galore.

"You know the routine. Mingle. There is a bar there in the foyer and another in the back yard, and handsome waiters everywhere to assist you. Tyler, the arrangements you sent over are the best ever. You outdid yourself this year, honey," as she kissed him on the cheek.

"It was easy. You inspire me."

Then so only Tyler could hear her, "Thank you for the discount. At your cost?"

"It's my pleasure, Carmella. Thank you for all you do for the community."

"Have fun, kids. That is the only thing on the agenda. I'm off to check on the caterer."

Carmella had a heart of gold. A long-time champion for human rights, she loved any excuse to have a party to raise money for her current worthy cause. She had gone through a very public, bitter divorce when her husband left her for a much younger woman. Nonetheless, Carmella weathered that difficult chapter with class and dedicated her life to philanthropy. She once confided to Tyler, "I'm not angry or bitter anymore toward my ex. I'd even invite him and his girlfriend to my fundraisers, but he's broke. I took all his money when he left." And then she laughed her hearty laugh. Since all of that transpired, Carmella had found a younger man who adored her and she him. "I'll never marry again, though. Been there, done that. Marriage is highly overrated if you ask me." And that was that as far as Carmella was concerned.

Tyler, Magda, and Sophie made their way through the huge, sprawling estate commenting on the costumes, appetizers, and the seven piece band playing on the lanais near the pool.

"It will be amazing if no one ends up in the pool this year," commented Magda, "especially with the dancing right next to it."

"Who's that?" Tyler asked. He was referring to a couple he had never seen before. Dressed in a royal blue flapper's dress and mobster's suit, the couple was quite striking.

Sophie offered, "I think that their last name is Girrardi. They recently bought a huge place overlooking Lake Michigan in Ludington. He's a CEO of some big company. They just moved here a few weeks ago."

"How do you know all of that?" Tyler queried.

"I keep my ears open, and I get around," Sophie replied with a mysterious grin. "But really, that's all I know."

"She looks like a cheerleader who married the captain of the football team."

"Aren't you the intuitive one! I dare say you are correct. They look like the Roaring Twenties version of Ken and Barbie."

Suddenly Tyler stopped in his tracks. Across the room, he had spotted the Reverend Ben Thompson.

Sophie took Tyler's arm as she watched Ben and his wife. "He's a real shit, Tyler. Don't let his presence ruin your evening."

"I won't. I knew that he could very well be here."

Tyler quipped, "Her name is Jacqueline," using the French pronunciation. "Her name means 'one who supplants.'"

"It's a pity that she can't see through him," Magda thought. "I wonder if he is faithful."

"He might be able to spell the word on a good day. His ministry is a sham, and his life is a joke. You know that, Tyler," Sophie said.

"I do. My brain knows that. However, my heart still hasn't gotten that memo. But enough of that." Raising his glass, "To the evening and Carmella's fabulous party."

"To the evening!" Magda and Sophie chimed in.

"I'm going to go see who is playing the ivories at the baby grand. Hopefully he/she knows a few songs from my repertoire." Magda loved to sing.

"Let's go dance, Tyler, and show them how it's done."

"Go ahead, Sophie. I will be there shortly." His gaze returned to Ben, and Tyler's memories took him back even farther than he had gone for a very long time.

CHAPTER TWO

Ben was coming over for dinner tonight, like he had once a week for six months. Tyler loved to cook, and Ben seemed to love everything Tyler prepared for him. Tonight was going to be a special evening: candles, a good bottle of cabernet sauvignon, coq au vin with a chocolate raspberry cake, Ben's favorite, for dessert.

Tyler remembered so clearly the night they met. Out of the blue, he attended a Lenten service at the Church of the Open Door in Pentwater on an Ash Wednesday. Reverend Ben wove into the sermon, which was really just a talk, how he had recently ended his marriage and was adjusting to being single again and how strange that all seemed to him. It wasn't about dating again but rather, just coming home to an empty home and dining alone. Tyler thought that it was brave for the handsome Reverend Ben to announce that news from the pulpit. Tyler glanced around at the sparse crowd. No one else seemed to be moved by that or the rest of the sermon, which dealt with conquering fears and empowering one's self. He quoted Eckhart Tolle's work that spoke about the fact that the word "sin" had been greatly misunderstood and misinterpreted. The word "sin" really meant "to miss the mark" so that in reality, to sin meant that one was missing the point of human existence. One who misses the mark is living unsuccessfully and will suffer and cause suffering. Not your typical "I'm a sinner so I'm going to wear ashes on my forehead fare."

Reverend Ben closed by stating, "So if you are missing the mark, then you alone have the power and ability to change that. As that wise leader Mahatma Gandi told us, 'Be the change you wish to see in the world.'"

Metaphysically speaking, there are no coincidences. Tyler liked what this minister said and knew he was here for a reason.

When the service was over, Rev. Ben was in the narthex greeting those in attendance, shaking hands, smiling, doing what was expected of one in that position. The six-foot tall minister looked handsome in his charcoal gray suit, accented with a red tie. *Red for power,* Tyler thought. There seemed to be a few more older, unaccompanied women than couples present this evening. *Isn't that interesting?*

As the crowd ahead of him dispersed, Tyler's turn came to greet Reverend Ben. "You don't know me, but I thought that it was particularly brave of you to announce your impending divorce from the pulpit. Not many people would have done that."

Reverend Ben's dark blue eyes fixated on Tyler's hazel eyes. "Thank you. I just thought better to say it once and have it over with. And you're right, I don't know you, but I need to.

"I'm Tyler. Tyler from Pentwater."

"Tyler from Pentwater. I like your teal-colored shirt, Tyler."

Taking Reverend Ben's hand and holding it, "You need to know and to believe that you will get through all of this, and it will be okay."

"That is the kindest thing anyone has said to me. For some reason, there's some myth, some stigma, that a minister shouldn't get divorced."

"Well, I wouldn't know about that. But when something is over, it's over. Better to leave and move on than to stay and be miserable. It was nice meeting you."

"You, too, Tyler. Hope you come back."

Tyler could not help but intuit that this man was gay, closeted and gay, and that is why his marriage ended. Tyler's intuition was seldom wrong, and his gaydar was never off. It just came to him. He didn't have to force it.

Tyler started attending the Church of the Open Door fairly regularly. He looked forward to the uplifting talks. They were not sermons. Sermons were preachy. Reverend Ben always had something positive to say about moving forward through life's trials and challenges.

"As you go through your day and maybe you're dog-tired, but still find the energy to smile and say hello to that stranger in the mall, or on the busy sidewalk, you may encounter. You undoubtedly will have no idea how your smile and greeting may positively impact that person in some manner. I ask you to try it sometime. Trust me, you'll be glad you did."

Tyler liked that and liked Reverend Ben. It wasn't long and the good Reverend suggested that they have lunch and get to know one another better. Being self-employed and quite busy at the floral shop, Tyler never took much of a lunch break and couldn't really count on a definite time to eat. "Why don't you come over for dinner instead? I'm not a bad cook. Call me, and we'll set a date."

"I will."

The next day, Reverend Ben called and agreed to come over to Tyler's that coming Saturday at 6:00 p.m. Tyler closed the shop at noon on Saturdays, so he'd have time to leisurely fix a nice meal. He'd grill fresh salmon on cedar planks, have a salad and wine. He went to the Farmer's Market and bought the freshest ingredients for this dinner. He liked Ben a lot. He seemed to be a kind and genuine man. Tyler wanted this dinner to be special.

Ben showed up promptly at six wearing a pair of new tight-fitting jeans and a light blue sport shirt. In his right hand he carried a bottle of red wine.

"For you," he said, handing the wine to Tyler.

"Thanks. We can have this with dinner as long as you're not a purist and can only drink white wine with fish and red with beef. I'm going to grill the salmon. So, here's a corkscrew. Do you mind opening the wine, Reverend Ben?"

"Please just call me Ben, here and at church. I'm just Ben."

"Okay. Sure. Let me get glasses." Ben poured the cabernet sauvignon into the glasses, and they toasted to each other's friendship.

"So give me the grand tour, will you?" Ben was eager to see all of Tyler's house and seemed genuinely interested in each and every item. Tyler was fond of gemstones and had lots of large amethyst geodes throughout. Ben picked each piece up and admired it closely.

"Why do you have so much amethyst?"

"I like it, and its energy lends itself to healing, intuition, clairvoyance and besides, these gems from Mother Earth are so beautiful."

"May I hold this piece, Tyler?" Ben asked before picking up a tall piece known as a 'cathedral cut.'

"Yes. Can you feel the energy it has?"

"It's amazing. I see why you like it so much."

Tyler knew then that he would be giving a special piece from his collection to Ben one day. He was struck by Ben's appreciation of the purple gemstones.

Dinner went smoothly. They talked about each other's life experiences, what had brought them to Pentwater, Michigan. Tyler opened the second bottle of wine. They sat across the table from each other. Ben was practically on the edge of his seat, intently looking at Tyler, constantly, drinking in everything that he said. Tyler had never felt such interest from another man since Hank, but that was of a different nature. His relationship with Hank morphed into one of father/son, and Hank and Tyler grew to love each other in that sense. But the intense look from Ben's eyes conveyed something totally different. *That just confirms what I surmised about his marriage ending,* thought Tyler. Though Ben was quick to volunteer that he and his ex-wife just grew apart and to stay married would only mean cohabitating under the same roof. There were no third parties, no drug issues, no money issues, or any truth to the rumor that Ben was gay.

"Really? I haven't heard any rumors about you."

"That's good, but just in case you had, I wanted you to know."

I wonder why he told me that? mused Tyler to himself.

When dinner was over and the candles nearly burned out, it was almost 10:00 p.m. Ben excused himself saying that he needed to be bright-eyed in the morning for church. Tyler went to shake his hand goodbye, and Ben said, "No, we're beyond that. We can hug. Okay?" Ben was about 6'1" to Tyler's 5'10". He pulled Tyler into him and rested his chin on Tyler's shoulder and pressed his face tightly next to Tyler's. Ben squeezed Tyler tightly and held the embrace a little longer than your average hug. *How long was an average hug, anyway?* Tyler had never timed one. *Was this the wine talking?* Tyler couldn't see the warm smile on Ben's face as he held Tyler tightly to him. Both men just knew it felt good to be held.

"See you in church tomorrow morning?"

"Sure."

Tyler went to church the next morning. What the topic was he couldn't really say. He kept replaying the events of the night before over in his mind. When the service was over, Tyler went to shake hands with Ben, but Ben, who had been hugging others as well, pulled Tyler into his body, into his personal space to hug him. He hugged him just as tightly, just as closely as the night before. *Now, I know I'm not imagining this, and neither of us is under the influence of wine,* Tyler thought to himself. Tyler looked at others around him to see if anyone was looking or staring at the two men embracing. No one that he could see. So the newly-single minister was closely hugging the openly-gay guy. Imagine that.

And so it went. A few weeks later, there was an appetizer and wine gathering in the church parlor. It was a "meet and greet" opportunity for members of the congregation to relax and get to know each other and to meet newcomers. This congregation, or community, as they liked to refer to themselves obviously liked any excuse to party. "Just bring a bottle of wine and an appetizer to share." Ben made it a point to encourage Tyler to attend. He sent Tyler two, no make that four, emails reminding him of the event and stating emphatically that he expected to see him there.

I don't know. It's a Friday evening, and I'm usually pretty tired by then. But Tyler went because Ben insisted. He could thaw out a bag of shrimp and bring some wine. Not hard.

When Tyler arrived, there were already about 75-100 people at the church parlor. The community was growing. Some were new to him, others he knew from town, and some from attending services the last few weeks.

"Red's on this table, white's on that one. Appetizers go over there. Oh, shrimp, great. No one else has brought any so far." Ben was busy mingling with everyone and didn't say anything other than a "hello, glad you could make it" to Tyler. *And what did you expect, Tyler Reynolds?* he thought to himself. The event was from 7-9:00 and by 8:30, Tyler had had enough small talk and went to retrieve his shrimp platter. As he was picking it up, Ben came up to him.

"Leaving already? I haven't had a chance to talk to you."

Tyler suddenly felt his energy and his emotions buoyed up as Ben focused his smile and attention on him. And if the truth were known, Ben felt just as happy to be able to talk to Tyler one-on-one. It had been a long day for the Reverend Ben, but suddenly he wasn't tired anymore. He could be himself with Tyler.

"You've been busy. Why don't you finish these last two shrimp so I don't have to throw them out?"

Ben did, and Tyler set the plate down. They made small talk, and then Ben hugged Tyler, laughing so that anyone else would think that they were sharing a joke.

"I am really glad that you came here tonight, Tyler. You made my day."

"It was great seeing you, too, Ben. It's nice to see you socially, and not just on Sunday."

Ben hugged him again.

"Well, I have had a long day, and I'm going home, Ben."

"Take some of this wine with you."

"You don't really think that I'm driving with open wine bottles in my car do you? That would not be wise." Then flirtatiously, "I could be pulled over and possibly arrested. Whoever would I call to come bail me out of jail?"

Ben, taking the bait, and raising his right hand, "That would be me. You can always depend on me, Tyler."

Smiling, "That's good to know, but I'm still not taking any wine home with me."

"Let me give you a hug goodbye." Ben hugged Tyler so closely and so tightly that Tyler started to get hard. Then Ben whispered into Tyler's ear, "I love you."

Tyler broke the hug, looked at a beaming, radiant Ben and said, "I feel the same way about you."

"I'll see you soon."

"Okay. Sure thing."

Tyler all but floated out of the church parlor as he headed to his car. *I feel like Eliza Doolittle. I could have danced all night!!*

Tyler climbed into his silver SUV, put the key in the ignition, and sat there glowing. *Ben loves me. He actually told me that he loves me!*

CHAPTER THREE

It was a Saturday morning in early April. Tyler was cleaning out the flower beds around his house and was working in the back yard. It was tedious work raking the dead oak leaves from last fall into piles, but Tyler was humming show tunes to make the job go faster. At least that is what he told himself. The leaves were cold, wet, and yucky to the touch, so he wore gloves as he scooped them into the small garbage can and then dumped them into the larger paper yard waste bags that the city demanded be used. Only then would the service haul them away during the first full week of the month. Since the leaves were wet and heavy from the melted snow, one couldn't fill the bags very full or else they would tear apart from the weight and then you would have to get another bag and start all over again.

Ben had stopped in at the floral shop only to be told by Sophie this was Tyler's Saturday off. Sophie thought Ben would have known that since Tyler kept her appraised of every word, every hug, every gesture that the Reverend Ben Thompson conveyed to Tyler. She didn't know why, but she was skeptical of Ben's actions and intentions toward Tyler. It was a strong vibe that she felt. Something was not quite right with him. She stated that fact to Tyler on more than one occasion. At Tyler's insistence, Sophie had accompanied him to Sunday services on two occasions. "It just doesn't speak to me, as it does to you, Tyler. But if you like attending here, then, by all means, go for it. But are you attending because of what is being said from the pulpit or are you so memorized by Ben's good looks, that you have lost sight of what is happening here?" Sophie obviously thought that Ben was hiding something behind his smile. *There is a sadness in his eyes. I wonder why Tyler can't see it?* However, Sophie was wise enough in her own right to know that Tyler had to discover it and not merely be told to beware.

"That's right. I guess it slipped my mind."

Ben walked through the gate into Tyler's back yard. "I thought you had a wedding to officiate today, Ben."

"It's later this afternoon, so I stopped by to see what you're up to."

Tyler nodded toward a half-filled bag, "Up to my ass in last year's leaves. If you don't mind getting your hands dirty, you could assist by holding the bags open while I fill them."

Ben was eager to help out, and the work went twice as fast. Ben found a pair of work gloves in the garage and started to rake leaves as well. By noon, the job was finished, and Tyler was grateful for the help and company. He made sandwiches for their lunch. Holding up a bottle of merlot that Ben had brought over earlier he asked, "A glass of wine with lunch?" "Just one glass for me. We wouldn't want the minister to appear under the influence at the wedding, would we?"

When it was time for Ben to leave, he hugged Tyler as always, tight and long. As the embrace broke, Tyler got a burst of courage and asked, "Ben, do you remember what you said to me at the end of the wine and appetizer party at church?"

"No, not really."

"You don't? Really?"

"Oh, yeah. I said I loved you."

"What exactly did you mean by that?"

"Tyler, I love you." Ben stared at Tyler intently.

"Okay. I just need to know."

After an awkward pause, Ben hurriedly added, "I don't love you in a romantic sense. But I just love you. I love you very much."

"Oh."

Tyler's mind was racing. *He holds me, embraces me as though we are lovers both in public and in private, whispers so no one else around can hear him say "I love you" and doesn't mean that in a romantic sense. What other sense is there in that setting, in that context?*

"Just thought I'd ask."

"Not a problem. See you in church tomorrow?"

"Probably."

Denial is not a river in Egypt. That's what Tyler wanted so much to say to this conflicted man. However, he thought better of it. Ben was finding his way. Tyler would give him some time, and it would all be good. All was in Divine Order.

That evening, Tyler was having dinner with good friends, Dennis and Michael, and he shared the day's events. "Mary, that man is so far in the closet that it's a wonder he hasn't suffocated. No straight man hugs another man the way he hugs you. I've seen him." Dennis was emphatic.

"That's right, *mon ami*. No straight man whispers into another man's ear that he loves him so that the others around can't hear him. Because love for one's brother or for one's country or hell, even love for chocolate is not the kind of love that one whispers about. And that is all I have to say about it. There. Finished and done!" as Michael closed the conversation.

Tyler agreed. He knew he was falling in love with the handsome minister. He would have to give Ben more time.

Tyler hadn't set the alarm for Sunday morning. He got up early after a restless night and decided to go to church anyway. After the service, Ben hugged him as always and said, "You know, I felt really good yesterday. Working in the yard with you, lunch, some wine. The wedding went well. I went to the dinner and reception, had a couple of more glasses of wine and went home and slept really well."

"Good for you, Ben. I'm glad. Thank you again for your help with the leaves."

When Tyler got home, he checked his email. Usually, he did so upon rising but for some reason today, he hadn't done so. There was an email from Ben sent at 4:00 a.m. "Had a good night's sleep, huh? Not if you're up emailing at 4:00 in the morning."

It read, "Tyler, thanks for asking the question about my intentions yesterday. I didn't find it offensive or off-putting in any way. If there is one thing that I'm certain about, it is my sexual orientation, just as you are certain about yours. In fact, I'm known for often joking about how heterosexual I am! I hope our embraces and closeness can continue. See you in church later today? Ben."

Tyler sat there staring at the computer screen as he re-read Ben's message. "Who the fuck jokes about how heterosexual he is? Especially a minister? Oh, my God, does this man have issues or what?"

And so it went. Ben continued to spend more and more time with Tyler each week. However, they always met at Tyler's house. He had suggested a couple of times that he could come to Ben's and cook dinner there. "But your house is so inviting, so comfortable, Tyler." After awhile, Tyler let it go. The important thing was they obviously enjoyed each other's company. They talked about lots of subjects: travel, the world, films, theater. They ate well, and they drank lots of red wine. Tyler became more involved with the

Church of the Open Door. He started to usher on Sundays and began to willingly tithe. Because Tyler was doing well at the floral shop, the Church of the Open Door reaped the rewards. Tyler was well thought of in the community and seemed to be loved by the other church members. Or so he believed at the time. If this is what it took for Ben to come around to admit to himself and to Tyler that he was gay, Tyler didn't seem to mind. In addition to tithing, Tyler made sure there were two beautiful fresh floral arrangements on the altar every Sunday.

Tyler was really a Spiritualist at heart. He believed in the communication with those who had already crossed over for one thing. His connection and friendship with Magda and Sophie enhanced his belief system. In addition, he had long thought of himself as spiritual but not religious for years. He didn't like the dogma or control issues that came with organized religion. It was too restrictive and too limiting. But the Church of the Open Door was different. He would find out later that basically it wasn't.

Ben was fascinated with Tyler's metaphysical knowledge. One night after dinner he asked, "What happens when you give a reading? What do you mean by energy work? Energy healing? The term light worker?"

Tyler explained in laymen's terms what he was asked. As for a reading, all mediums are psychic. Not all psychics are mediums. A medium is a person who can connect with the spirit energy of those who have crossed over to the other side. Some see, some hear, some smell, some taste, or some have a combination of those gifts. Those are what are known as the clairs. There is clairvoyance, clairaudience, clairsentience, claircognizance and clairalience. A psychic can tune into the energy and predict things, tell you what you already know, give confirmation of what has happened, what is, and so forth. Mediums and psychics could call upon a variety of modalities to facilitate the reading. Some used tarot cards, astrology, psychometry, palms, tea leaves, flowers, flame, to mention a few. Tyler stressed that a reading was not, nor should ever be construed as fortune telling. It is a gift from the Divine, and most charge for their services, for their time. That is how they earn their living.

"Why don't they do it for free if it is a gift from the Divine?"

"Good question. But wouldn't you agree that Barbra Striesand's voice or the voices of the members of Il Divo are gifts from the Divine?"

"Yes."

"Would you expect them to not charge for their CD's, for their concerts? That is how they make their living. They are using the gifts that they were blessed with."

Eager to know more, Ben asked, "What about healing?"

"As for healing, there are several modalities. First and foremost, let me tell you that a healer is merely a facilitator for the Divine. Anyone who says "I healed so and so", beware of that person. Ego is involved there. Stay away." Tyler explained about what he had studied. Healing Touch, Reconnective Healing, Reiki, Ama-Deus were the more common ones. Each is a valid healing modality with its own unique approach to healing. But in each modality, the healer, or facilitator, is merely a conduit for the energy from the Divine and asks that it be sent to the place where the healing needs to go. The Light is never wrong and can't be sent to the wrong place. Sometimes the healer and/or the person being healed will feel energy: maybe cold, maybe heat, maybe nothing. He/she might see colors or might not see anything. He/she might not feel anything happening, but the healing is taking place and will continue for several hours or days as needed, long after their session has ended. The only requirement is to have an open mind.

"Did you realize that Jesus was a healer? He was taught by the Essenes, who raised him along with Mary and Joseph." Tyler loved sharing what he had learned.

Ben wanted to know it all. "What if the person wants to be healed of a terminal illness or some chronic condition, and it doesn't go away?"

"Then perhaps that person has a 'contract' with that situation and the universe to learn whatever he needs to learn and to teach those he comes in contact with what they need to know and learn. Maybe the healing is to make peace with the impending death of the physical body. Eventually, everyone's body dies, but the spirit, the soul, doesn't and goes on to experience the next chapter in that soul's journey to the next dimension. The Native Americans say that when a person's body has died, that soul has 'walked on.' I like that term a lot."

Ben was mesmerized. "So fascinating."

"Energy healing can work greatly in tandem with Western medicine. I would never tell someone to just go get a healing and cancel his doctor's appointment. No, utilize all the universe has to give you. I love talking about this and sharing what I have learned. Does this make any sense to you, or have I blown you away?"

"The reason I ask is that I have been having ever increasing pain in my right shoulder. It's getting so that it really is hard for me to put on a shirt. It's really brought my work outs to a grinding halt. I've had an MRI done, and I get the results on Monday. I'm concerned. And scared."

"That's understandable. Why haven't you said something sooner?"

"I guess I thought it would go away. I just wanted to be strong and tough."

"There's nothing weak about admitting you are in pain."

"Tyler, would you try your healing technique on me? Please."

"Certainly."

"When can I schedule a healing session with you?"

"Tomorrow?"

CHAPTER FOUR

Ben came to see Tyler the following Tuesday evening for a healing session. He had been having trouble with his right shoulder for a couple of months now. Ben thought that he had injured it lifting weights at the gym. He was very proud of his pectoral muscles and his baseball biceps and liked to wear tight-fitting tee shirts whenever possible to show off his many hours of hard work at the gym. Ben had tried a combination of ibuprofen and ointments, but the pain didn't go away. His doctor said he would need surgery to correct the matter.

"What do you have to lose? Try this before you agree to go under the knife." Ben arrived fifteen minutes early clad in old, tight-fitting jeans and a blue-and-white plaid short sleeve shirt. Once inside Tyler's house, he kicked off his sandals and was barefoot. Tyler had already set up the massage table in his meditation room. Candles were burning, and relaxing, soothing music was playing.

"What should I expect? What's going to happen?"

"I'm going to have you start by lying face down. I'm going to open with a silent prayer to the Divine and ask that the Light be directed to the area of your body that is causing the discomfort. I will scan your body first and lightly place my hands on the areas that I intuit need it. Do I have permission to touch you?"

"Certainly."

"Then I will more than likely focus on the back of your right shoulder. When I'm 'told' it's time, I will nudge you, gently ask you to turn over, and rest on your back, so I can send healing to the front. When that is done, I would like to gently massage your shoulder. I have lavender infused healing oils to use. Is that okay with you?"

"Yes, of course."

"Feel free to close your eyes, zone out, whatever and where ever Spirit takes you during this healing journey. We can talk about it later if you want to."

"If you're going to massage me, I should just take my shirt off now."

"That isn't neces—"

"You'll have to help me. It was all I could do to get dressed to come over here. I didn't take any meds because I wanted to see what kind of effect the healing might have on me." Ben stared intently at Tyler but made no move to start unbuttoning his shirt. Focusing on each button, Tyler deftly unbuttoned the shirt and opened it, revealing Ben's well-defined pectorals and six-pack abs. There was the absolutely perfect placement of dark chest hair with a treasure trail leading down to his navel. *Damn! I knew he worked out but I didn't really think that I would see an Adonis who could be on the cover of Men's Fitness magazine.* Tyler helped Ben removed his shirt, first freeing up the left arm and shoulder, then slipping it off the ailing right side. *My God! This wasn't going to be easy.*

"Ready? You need to lie face down on the table. Let me adjust the cradle so that your head and neck are comfortable."

Tyler called in his guides, his healing angels, as well as calling on the big guns, Archangel Michael and Archangel Raphael. As always, he asked to be a conduit for this man, to send the healing where it was needed. He proceeded to scan his body with his hands. *"Alleluia"* was playing softly in the CD player. Tyler didn't sense any particular blockages in the alleged affected area, but he did feel some incredible heat in that area as he worked at helping Ben release the discomfort from his body. He scanned Ben's body again, his hands hovering closely over him. Unbeknownst to Tyler, Ben closed his eyes and was smiling a kind of "Mona Lisa" smile. After approximately twenty minutes, Tyler whispered softly in Ben's ear to turn over. Ben did so without opening his eyes. Tyler adjusted the pillow under his head and placed a cushion under Ben's legs for additional support. He repeated the scan on the front.

Why do you have to be so handsome, Ben? Tyler asked himself. *Focus, Tyler. Ben came here for a healing, not to get laid.* "Oh, did he really?" Sophie responded when Tyler later told her about the session.

Tyler didn't sense anything physically wrong with Ben. He noticed great warmth when he placed his hands on Ben's forehead as well as the heart chakra area. It appeared that he needed to deal with stuff that he was suppressing, and the pain from not doing so was manifesting in his arm and shoulder. After a few minutes, Tyler put some of the lavender scented oil in his palms to warm it. He then gently started to massage the shoulder area, placing his right hand under Ben's shoulder and then using his left to massage and gently rub the front side and the top of his arm. With his eyes still closed, Ben automatically raised his body slightly to accommodate the movement. Tyler automatically massaged each of Ben's arms, gently caressing his muscular biceps with his finger tips. First the right arm, then the left. He couldn't help but notice that the bulge in Ben's jeans was growing. Tyler moved his hands over Ben's pectoral muscles, his finger tips lightly grazing Ben's dark brown nipples. God, how Tyler wanted to yank those jeans off of him and just go down on him in one fell swoop. *Stop it, Tyler.*

But he couldn't. No, Tyler would not do anything unethical like that. There were enough charlatans out there in the world already giving energy work a bad name.

"I'm going to massage your feet, Ben. Hope you're not ticklish."

"No, don't. My feet are dirty."

"Oh, please. I'll wash my hands when I'm done. There are trigger points in the feet that affect the rest of the body."

Tyler moved to the foot of the table and pushed up the pant leg to just above Ben's calf. He then gently massaged the calf, working down to the foot and working on the sole of the foot, gently releasing all of the pent-up tension. First, he massaged the left calf, then the right.

When finished, Tyler moved to the side of the table and took Ben's hands in his and squeezed them to let him know the session was over. He helped Ben sit up slowly. Ben swung his legs around to the side and let them dangle off of the table. Without letting go of Tyler, he just leaned forward and rested his forehead on Tyler's, third eye to third eye. Tyler had NEVER had anyone act like this before at the conclusion of a healing session.

After a few moments of silence, Ben asked, "What did you intuit about my body, about my shoulder?"

"I'm not a doctor, but I didn't intuit any blockages or any injured areas. I think that there is something on your emotional plane, your mental plane that you need to address and make peace with to facilitate this healing. Know that the healing energy will continue to work with you for the next three days. What did you sense?"

"I saw colors. Some purples, lots of blues, some greens."

"I called in Archangel Michael; his color is blue. I called in Archangel Raphael. His color is green. Good."

"I felt such peace. Sometimes I felt you touch me, and sometimes I didn't, even though I knew you were. Bizarre." Both men were silent a moment. Ben broke the quiet, "I didn't bring my checkbook, but I feel that I should compensate you."

"I don't charge for healing. If you want to donate some money, then you can give a love offering to the Human Rights Campaign. Besides, if I charged you for what this is worth, you probably couldn't afford it," Tyler chuckled.

"You're probably right about that. THANK YOU!"

Ben hugged Tyler again, holding him closer than ever, not wanting to let him go.

A couple of weeks later, Ben reported that his shoulder was somewhat better but not perfect. Tyler had just returned from taking a weekend seminar on Reconnective Healing and wanted to use it on Ben. Eagerly, Ben came over the very next day.

"Should I take my shirt off right away?"

"Actually, you can leave it on. This is a different healing modality. I'm not going to touch you. If by chance I do touch you, I will whisper to you that it's me."

"Tyler, it's okay if you touch me. I don't mind."

"I know, but that's not how this is going to work today. So if you feel that someone has touched you, you will know you have been touched by Spirit."

"Is this modality better than the others you practice?"

"I wouldn't say better, just different. I took the class because I wanted one more tool to add to my toolbox."

Tyler facilitated the session, no music this time, just the sound of the air conditioning when it kicked on.

Again, Ben reported seeing colors and feeling at peace. "And I know that you touched me several times."

"No, that was not me."

"Well, something did!"

Ben was pain-free from then on and never went to see the doctor about that issue again.

It was sometime later when Tyler was having a reading done for him by Magda, that she said, "When you conduct healing sessions, you pull out parts of all of the healing modalities that you have learned, don't you? You don't stick to only one."

"It's all from the Divine, so I take the best aspect of each one. I use what I resonate with from each and use it accordingly, and it seems to work for people. I know the energy is flowing through me, and sometimes I feel like I get a healing whenever I give one. And that's that."

Magda went on with the reading. She never used "props" as she called them. She merely repeated, or channeled, what she was seeing and/or hearing with her sixth sense, her "clairs." "I'm seeing a Phoenix for you. You are familiar with the legend of the Phoenix, are you not?"

"Somewhat."

She elaborated, "The Phoenix is a mythical bird that periodically consumes itself in flames and then emerges reborn from its own ashes. Sometimes we refer to our tests, our challenges in life as initiations or trials by fire, metaphorically speaking, when they are that intense. We all experience them on many levels. It is in going through these 'tests', if you will, that our soul grows."

"Yes, I understand."

"Tyler, you know that a true medium only gives messages from Spirit with love. Doom and gloom messages are given from fear. I don't do the latter."

"I know that, Magda. What are you trying to tell me?"

"I cannot sugar coat this, not for you. You are going to be given what you think is more than your fair share of 'challenges' or 'tests.' Never forget that you won't be handed anything that you can't handle, Tyler. You have the resources within and without. Do not lose sight of that. You have come through many challenges already in your relatively young life. You are on an accelerated path. The energies in the universe are intensifying. Those on this path know that it isn't always an easy one. But for us, there is no alternative. You chose this when you incarnated in this lifetime."

"Yes."

"I'm seeing a ship on stormy seas. It is been tossed about from high wave to high wave. Then the waters are calm. You're going to go through a rough patch in relationships. You will know great heartache, and conversely, great love. There is the love that you have been looking for coming to you, but not just yet."

Tyler's mind was racing. He thought that Ben was the love of his life. Certainly, they were soul mates. That fact had been confirmed in a previous reading. Ben just needed time to come out. He was sure that Ben loved him as much as he did Ben.

Magda paused as if listening to Spirit. "You will always have enough money in this lifetime. You don't want for anything now, nor will you ever."

"I've never worried about money. Not anymore. I've always trusted that I would have what I need."

Magda paused as she was continuing to listen to Spirit. "The Phoenix comes for you, Tyler. And like this Phoenix, you are a survivor! Always remember that." She paused, "There is great love for you here." With that, Magda came out of her trance.

"That was intense," was all Tyler could say. But what did it all mean? He thought things were going very well. They certainly were at work and with Ben, too. He had noticed how Ben seemed to always work into his sermons references to our "LGBT brothers and sisters and equal rights for everyone." Most assuredly he was paving the path for announcing that he was a gay man and in a healthy, loving relationship. *But when would this happen? How much longer would he have to wait?* Tyler wondered.

CHAPTER FIVE

Ben continued to see Tyler at least twice a week. Tyler willingly became much more involved at the church not only because he believed in it, but because it was important to Ben, and it would bring them closer together. Ben would always come for dinner on either Friday or Saturday evening and see Tyler at least once earlier in the week. He usually prefaced it with church business as the reason, but that never remained the topic for long. Ben always sat next to Tyler on the sofa, knees and legs touching, and always looked deep into Tyler's hazel eyes with his misty blue ones. Tyler couldn't help but think that there was such a sadness behind those misty blue eyes and behind his smile. Ben always had a smile for everyone. It was as if he didn't want anyone to know what was going on deep inside his mind or heart. However, Tyler knew. He listened to his guides, and he always trusted what he heard implicitly.

Tyler had been asked to be on a committee that would work on a pledge drive to get the members to pledge a substantial amount to be paid over a three-year period. This amount was over and above what members were already contributing. It wouldn't be an easy sell, but Ben and the Board firmly believed that if the Church of the Open Door was to move forward, the astronomical debt that had accrued over time must be eliminated as quickly as possible so that the church could start channeling that money to do some really good things for the less fortunate. The list of agencies in need was growing. Tyler truly believed in what was being said weekly from the pulpit. Ben continued to make it a point to mention how members of the LGBT community were not second-class citizens and were always welcome there, too. Tyler felt proud to be a part of this, and he felt good that he was accepted here. His contributions, fiscal and non-fiscal, were appreciated. Tyler gave generously of his time and talent. He was always the first to sign up for any activity, whether it was to raise funds or just have fun. He helped to decorate, prepare refreshments, or any other way that he could be of assistance. It felt good inside to be giving from the heart.

Ben came over one afternoon to meet with Tyler about his part of the committee work. Tyler had left work early to meet with Ben since Ben said it was so important that they do so. Ben plunged right in. How much money would Tyler be pledging?

"Ben, I haven't decided yet how much I'm going to pledge. I thought that I had another week before I have to turn that in."

"You do, but I didn't want you to feel taken for granted, so I wanted to talk to you, the way you are going to talk to others who need an encouraging word."

As Ben started to go through the monologue about the importance of what Church of the Open Door was doing, Tyler stopped him.

"Ben, I'm on the committee. I believe in this work. You're really preaching to the choir on this one."

"I am. Sorry. It's just that—well, this is the amount that I pledged," pointing to the $15,000 column, "and I would hope you do, too."

Tyler was slightly annoyed but he suppressed it. Ben was just doing what he felt he needed to do.

"I will make up my mind about the amount and turn in my pledge card by the end of the week. I'll do what I can." *But I'm not going to go into hock and get carried away by pledging more than I can really afford,* he thought to himself.

Tyler switched the conversation to creative visualization. "See the amount needed and more as already pledged. Don't put a dollar amount on it. If we need $500,000, then say we have all the money we need. We have more than the amount needed. That way the universe will bring abundance, but you're limiting yourself if you tell the Universe you only need so much. Because then that is all the universe will deliver. You need to always think in terms of abundance. Don't limit yourself."

"Tyler, I love your outlook." He took Tyler into his arms and held him very tightly. His face pressed tightly against Tyler's cheek.

Tyler's heart was racing. Tyler thought, *Okay, I can't hold back any longer.* He kissed Ben on the side of his face next to his ear. Ben responded in kind by pressing his full lips against Tyler's cheek. Tyler then moved his lips to the middle of Ben's right cheek and kissed that spot slowly. Again, Ben followed suit, kissing Tyler's right cheek. Then Tyler kissed Ben slowly on the corner of his mouth. Ben kissed Tyler on the corner of his mouth. The touch of Ben's soft, full lips on Tyler's face got him instantly aroused. Tyler had never known such tenderness. He kissed Ben firmly on his lips, savoring the touch, the warmth. Then he felt Ben slowly, gently push his tongue into Tyler's mouth. Tyler willingly took Ben's eager tongue deep into his mouth, responding in kind. They continued kissing like this for several minutes.

Tyler unbuttoned Ben's shirt and ran his fingers over his chiseled chest. His mouth found Ben's dark quarter-sized nipples, and he gently started sucking on them. Ben moaned. Not exactly sure what to do, he followed suit. He unbuttoned Tyler's shirt and pulled his tee shirt off over his head and devoured his nipples as well. "Don't be rough, baby. Just nurse on them. I love that."

"Sorry, I didn't mean to be so rough."

Tyler took Ben by the hand and led him to the bedroom. They frantically undressed each other, kissing each other all over. Ben yanked his jeans off; his throbbing manhood too big for the boxer briefs confining it. Tyler tongued Ben's member through the fabric, then put his teeth on the waistband, pulling it back and with his hands on each side of Ben's hips, slid those briefs off, and allowed Ben's large circumsized penis the freedom it demanded. Ben climbed onto Tyler's bed while Tyler hastily removed his own clothing, except for his socks. *I guess he wants to try and knock those off,* Tyler laughed to himself. The two horny men were all over each other in the bed licking, kissing, caressing every inch of each other. Tyler couldn't stand it and started to deep throat Ben without stopping.

Ben cried out.

Tyler hunkered down, and Ben blasted his load deep into Tyler's willing hot mouth and throat. "Please stop. It's so sensitive." Tyler showed no mercy and kept his mouth on Ben until Ben was through ejaculating and went limp.

"Oh, my God. That was awesome."

Ben proceeded to give Tyler a hand job, bringing him to climax while kissing him passionately. Tyler really thought that Ben would have reciprocated what he had done for him, but Ben didn't. *Well, he will next time.* The men lay in each other's arms for about a half hour, saying nothing, savoring the afterglow. And so it went.

It went like that every week. They had the same sex two to three times a week. Ben never gave Tyler the kind of amazing attention that he received from him. Eventually, their relationship advanced to include anal sex, and Ben was only too eager to be the top man. When Tyler pulled out a box of condoms and lube, Ben said, "Condoms? I thought you were clean as I am."

"I am and am going to stay that way. But no glove, no love." Laughing, Ben suited up and they made passionate love.

Tyler was so in love with Ben. *It is only a matter of time before he admits to me and to himself, that he is gay, and that he loves me. I would marry you in a heartbeat, Ben. I am going to marry you.* These were the thoughts that occupied Tyler's mind the majority of his day. Tyler started visualizing that kind of life with the handsome minister everyone in the congregation adored. Little did they know, or even surmise, that when the Reverend Ben Thompson was visiting Tyler Reynolds on a regular basis, he was conducting his own selfish version of missionary work.

CHAPTER SIX

Life was good. Ben was at Tyler's house often. Tyler knew he finally had it all--a successful business and a handsome lover. He loved both passionately. Though sometimes Tyler wondered when Ben would say it was okay to go public with their relationship. Why wouldn't he? Ben continued to mention frequently in his Sunday sermons that the LGTB community deserved everyone's support and understanding. Surely he was just paving the way to come out. Why else would he speak so adamantly about this topic?

When Tyler told Sophie about his plans for the special dinner he planned for Ben she was somewhat skeptical. "Tyler, you know I love you and I want you to be happy. But have you ever asked yourself if Ben truly gets you? Does he really understand what you're all about?"

"What do you mean?"

"Other than me, you have kept the fact that you're intimate with him on a regular basis a secret from the rest of the world. That's not you. You're out. You're not in the closet. This isn't healthy for either of you."

"When Ben's ready, he will go public."

"It's not like he will lose his job over it. His church allegedly supports gay rights."

"I know what you're saying and you're right."

"It's not just that you have great sex together. Does he ever explore metaphysics or spirituality on the level that you and I do? I mean, if he's cool with it and loves you, then why doesn't he read about it and discuss it with you. All I ever her you talk about is what he says about his church."

"Hmmm."

"I'm just asking. I don't want you to be lead on or be blinded by his façade."

"Okay. Your point is well taken. Thank you for caring enough to say something." They hugged each other warmly.

Tyler knew in his heart that there was a lot of truth to what Sophie mentioned. However, no relationship was perfect and he wanted Ben to feel comfortable and come around when it was right for him to do so. *After all, Ben MUST love me or he wouldn't still be coming over.*

Ben always came to Tyler's house. Tyler mentioned a couple of times that he'd like to be invited over to Ben's place, especially since Ben often commented on how tasteful and welcoming Tyler's house was. "Maybe you can help me out with my place?"

"Sure, let me know when you want me to come over." That's as far as that topic ever went. Tyler had suggested going out to eat a various restaurants but Ben's response was always the same. "I prefer your home-cooked meals."

Today it was a year to the day that Ben first visited Tyler's house, had a long, leisurely dinner, and had admired everything throughout the house, especially the amethyst geodes. For this evening Tyler had made coq au vin, a salad with all of the freshest greens from the Farmer's Market, wine, and a chocolate raspberry cake, which was Ben's favorite.

When Ben walked into the dining room and saw the Waterford wine goblets, candles burning, and a beautiful floral centerpiece, he asked, "What's the special occasion?"

"It's our one-year anniversary."

"Anniversary? Of what? What are you talking about?" he asked as he sat down across the table from Tyler.

"It's a year ago today that we started seeing each other. I know it's not a year yet of when we started making love, but that can be another anniversary. Here, I got you something." Tyler handed a small wrapped box to Ben. It contained a ring made of white gold with small amethyst stones set across the top of the band. Rich, tasteful, but something a man could wear.

"Tyler, we need to talk."

"Open your gift first."

"Tyler, we can't do this anymore. *I* can't do this anymore."

"Do what anymore? I don't understand.

"This. Dinners. Sex. None of it." Ben paused, then took a deep breath. "I'm not going to see you any more. Only in church."

"What?" In an effort to be clever, a stunned, Tyler finally managed, "That's quite an announcement between the soup and the salad."

"I'm engaged. I'm getting married."

Tyler stared at Ben, not believing what he just heard.

"I'm engaged to a woman, a wonderful woman. I'm not going to do this anymore. I mean, really, after all, I'm a heterosexual."

"What the fuck! I'd laugh, but I'm not amused."

"I'm serious. We had our fun, but it's over. This isn't the kind of life I want for myself."

"What's wrong with this life? Tell me one thing that's wrong with it." A long silence was all that Ben spoke. "You can't, can you? You're an incredibly closeted gay man who obviously is currently oxygen-deprived. You're talking nonsense."

Again, Ben said nothing.

"Ben, I happen to be head over heels in love with you."

"I'm heterosexual."

"Ben, you hold me and you embrace me as though we are lovers, even in public."

"That's right. That's how I hug people."

"Not other men. I've watched you. Do you have any idea how many people have asked me what's going on between us when they see you hug me in public?"

"What do you tell them?"

"I say, Oh, that's just how Ben hugs me."

"You're right, that's how I hug everybody."

"Bullshit! Not everybody. I have been covering for you, lying for you all this time until you were ready to come out and live openly with me."

"Where did you ever get that idea? That I would fucking live with you?!"

"And then they tell me: One man doesn't hug another man the way he hugs you, unless there is more going on between the two of them. You want to know something, Ben? They're right. My straight male friends don't hug me that way."

"I'm heterosexual."

"You send me emails telling me that you miss me and are thinking of me. In the middle of the day, no less!"

"When I don't see you, I do miss you."

"A straight man doesn't do that."

"I'm heterosexual."

"You told me that you loved me. You whispered it in my ear."

"I'm a heterosexual."

"You made love to me in my bed. You kissed me like there was no tomorrow."

"Tyler, there's fucking, and then there's making love. Obviously you don't know the difference. We only fucked."

"I know who I am, Ben. I don't fall in love with straight men."

"I don't know how to respond to that."

"You could have said, 'gee, Tyler, I guess that there is always a first time for everything.' But you didn't."

"I'm a heterosexual."

"You keep saying that. But you know what, Ben? I'm really not the ONE you have to convince of THAT."

"I've known other gay guys. I never got this kind of shit from them."

"You asshole! Were you fucking them, too?"

Tyler was determined not to cry in front of Ben. "I'd leave now, but it's my house." Ben just stood there staring at Tyler. "That's your cue to get the fuck out of my house. And take this fucking cake with you. I made it for you."

Tyler shoved the oblong cake pan containing the chocolate raspberry cake into Ben's abdomen. "Go on. Take it!" Numb, Tyler walked over to the front door and held it open and gestured for Ben to leave. As Ben walked past him, he extended his right arm in an attempt to pull Tyler into him for a hug.

"No. I can't do that."

Tyler started to tremble, but forced himself to be strong. He followed Ben out the front door and stood on his front porch as he watched Ben go to his car. Ben opened the car door of his SUV and then turned to Tyler as if nothing out of the ordinary had happened.

"I hope that I continue to see you in Church."

"You need to leave now. Good-bye, Ben."

Tyler turned and went back into the house. He carefully closed the door, locked it, and sank to the floor sobbing. He hadn't cried this hard since he was a little boy. It was when his mother told him that his father had gone away, deserted them and would never be coming back. Except this time, Tyler was all alone.

CHAPTER SEVEN

Sophie had intended to go in to work early to tidy up the shop. Tyler had left early the day before so he could make the perfect dinner for the perfect evening with Ben. She couldn't wait to hear about it. However, there had been a rush of business later the previous day, and she hadn't left things as neatly and orderly as Tyler liked to leave everything at the day's end. She was tired and decided she'd go in an hour earlier than usual and clean up. She was surprised when she did get there at 7:00 a.m. to find Tyler already there and everything all cleaned up.

"I didn't think that you would beat me here this morning, Tyler. I'm sorry I left a mess. I fully intended to tidy up before you got here."

"Don't worry about it. It's not a big deal in the grand scheme of things. It's really nothing. I couldn't sleep, so I came in early."

It was then that Sophie took a good, long hard look at Tyler. He looked exhausted, body language very tight, constrained like he was holding back a floodgate of tears, a dam about to burst. "What's the matter? You look terrible, honey."

"I under-slept a little."

"This must be about Ben. Sit. Talk to me."

"Ben announced at the beginning of a fabulous dinner I had prepared that he is straight. He's getting married. To a woman."

"WHAT?"

"He can't see me anymore because suddenly the lack of oxygen in his closet has turned him back into a heterosexual."

"What prompted all of this after all of this time that you've been seeing each other?"

"I have no idea."

"He must have found someone gullible with money." Sophie always knew that there was something about the handsome minister that she didn't trust. But this?

"Maybe. I don't know. Maybe. Every time I said anything, his rote response was that he's a heterosexual. He told me that about seventeen times. He kept saying that over and over and over." The tears started to flow softly, slowly at first, then the dam let loose.

"What the fuck!? Who does that?"

"Exactly. I know that man better than he knows himself. He's about as straight as the fucking yellow brick road. I just thought I'd give him enough time, and he'd come out to himself at least, if not to me."

"I'm surprised that he ended it like this. I would have thought that he had a little more class."

"Apparently he's engaged. When did he have time to find some woman and bang her too? God damn it! I was faithful to him. It never entered my mind that this was how it was going to go. Lying fucking bastard! Mother-fucking hypocritical minister!" Tyler was red with rage. He had never felt so used, so betrayed. After all, he had given everything he had to offer to this man and to his church.

"That's pretty much how it went. I hope he chokes on that fucking cake. No, on second thought, I hope he eats all of it and then gains forty fucking pounds!"

"You ARE kidding me, aren't you? After all of that, you sent that dessert home with him? You could have brought it here. I like it, too, you know."

Shaking his head in disbelief, "What the fuck, Sophie? He and I are soul mates. I explained to him that we have had past lives together based on the regressions I've had done. This was our chance to complete that unfinished business. What soul mate does that to another soul mate?"

"You don't."

"He sent me an email this morning. Listen to this shit. 'Once again I remind you that I always have been and remain a heterosexual. As far as any physicality that was shared between us, I was merely expressing my humanity. I am owning what I can with this.'"

"Expressing his humanity? That wins the prize for euphemisms." Sophie shook her head.

"I feel so stupid. Didn't see this one coming. Did you or Magda?"

"Yes, Magda did. Remember what she told you about relationships in your last reading?"

"That's right. I forgot."

"You ARE a great intuitive. But you know as well as I do, that one can't read for himself. It doesn't work that way. We read for each other. We help each other heal. Don't beat yourself up."

"I loved him terribly, terribly. That's what is so sad. I didn't jump into bed with him right away either."

"Tyler, I know how much this hurts."

"Everybody leaves. They just leave. My dad walked out. My mother kicked me out. Hank died. Now, Ben. Everybody leaves."

Sophie took each of Tyler's hands in hers. "Look at me. Listen to me. I know that you're hurting. Give yourself permission to hurt, to feel the pain. That is the only way you will get through it. I'm here for you. So is Magda." Smiling, "We're not leaving you. You're stuck with us, like it or not."

"I know that. Thank you for reminding me."

"Tyler, I have never allowed stupid people to be a part of my life, and neither can you. If Ben is too fucking stupid to realize what a fine man you are, what a catch you are, if he's just too stupid for whatever reason, then I ask you: Do you want a stupid person in your life?"

"No, I suppose not."

"Of course, you don't. One day, I have no idea when that day is coming, but you will thank Ben for walking out. Someone so much better than you could possibly imagine will come into your life. I know this."

Tyler wanted to believe Sophie. In theory, he knew she was right, but he also knew his heart. No matter what Ben said or did, he would always love him. Always.

"Oh, I forgot to tell you this. As Ben, the alleged heterosexual, was getting into his car he says, 'See you in church.'" Sophie had never seen Tyler look so contemptuously disgusted.

Mirroring his scorn, "Now, I really hate him. I'm glad that I never started attending there, although I'm not judging you for doing so. But organized religion, even that place, that organization that prides itself on being like no other church, has just as much dogma, and just as much hypocritical bullshit. They keep telling everyone how inclusive they are, then they hold events at the country club with expensive admission prices. When I asked him about that, the Reverend Ben Thompson told me that inclusion didn't necessarily mean everybody all of the time. I wonder which dictionary he uses?"

Somewhat reluctantly Tyler said, "Go ahead. You can say it. Ben is a dick."

"Ben is a dick."

"Now you tell me. Thank you for listening to my sob story."

"Anytime, sweetie."

"Sophie, when you do the bookkeeping this morning, don't forget to create a bill for last week's flowers that I gave to the Church of the Open Door. I don't attend there anymore. Just bring it to me before you seal the envelope."

Tyler started to work on an arrangement that was to be delivered before noon. Sophie readied the bill and brought it to show Tyler for his approval. "That looks right." Tyler took a red ink pen and scribbled a note across the bottom of the statement. "Rev. Ben, enclosed please find the bill for flowers ordered and delivered to your organization. Business is business. Just expressing my humanity. Tyler." With that, he sealed the envelope and placed it with the other outgoing mail.

CHAPTER EIGHT

"Another glass of wine, sir? Perhaps, some champagne?" the waiter asked.

Suddenly, Tyler was jolted back into the reality of Carmella's lavish party. "Huh? Oh, sure. Um, a glass of white wine would be fine. Thank you."

How long had he been standing there lost in a past memory? *Well, I don't care. It is what it is.* He was still watching Ben and Jacqueline from across the crowded room. They seemed to be delighted to be there together, acting out their roles of lovers in love. *Well, I guess that's what they are. It should have been me with him tonight.* It had been six months since Ben ended it with Tyler. Yet Tyler kept thinking somewhere in his heart, somewhere in his brain, that Ben would come to his senses before it was too late, before he actually married her.

Tyler remembered the first time he met Jacqueline. She had come into the shop to arrange for flowers for their wedding. Tyler was filling out the form: bride's name, groom's name, etc. When she told him the groom was the Rev. Ben Thompson, he got a lump in his throat. "Ben recommended you. He said we had to get our flowers from you."

"Tell him thanks for the referral." Then Tyler told Jacqueline that he was going to let his assistant take over from there. She would be in good hands. He guaranteed they would be satisfied with the flowers.

Tyler went into the back room where Sophie was putting the final touches on a funeral arrangement. "I'll finish this. That woman out there is Ben's fiancé and has come to order flowers for their wedding. I can't wait on her. You take care of it, please. Oh, and Sophie, charge them an extra ten percent on everything they order. It can be your bonus."

"No, you're not going to do that. Besides, it won't change anything."

Once again, Tyler's memories took him back to the party. Ben and Jacqueline had moved away from the crowd to a corner of the huge room where they thought no one would notice them. Most people didn't, but Tyler's eyes were transfixed. Ben took Jacqueline into his arms and kissed her passionately and said, "Let's get out of here." Tyler could read his lips so clearly. As they left, they made their excuses to Carmella for leaving early.

Tyler's eyes watered. *They kissed sweetly, didn't they? God, he's never coming back to me is he? Tyler Reynolds, let this be your wake up call. You are NEVER, EVER going to let someone get that close to you again. You are not going to love someone that much again. 'As God is my witness,' thank you Scarlet O'Hara, I am never going to feel this way again. I am not going to let anyone into my heart again. It hurts too much. Besides, who said you HAVE to have someone special in your life? I am glad to say that no man needs me in his. That's just how it is.*

The tears flowed slowly down his cheek.

Tyler became aware of Magda's alto voice over the piano coming from the next room. She was singing "The Party's Over" from the show *Bells Are Ringing.* How appropriate. She always sang this song at the end of her set. It was her way of letting Tyler and Sophie know that when she was finished singing that song, she was ready to leave if they were.

Yes, the party was indeed over for Tyler and Ben. It was time to go home.

Unbeknownst to Tyler, someone was watching him through all of this. While his wife was somewhere else in the crowd, doing what she did best, schmoozing, Christopher Girrardi, a keen observer of human nature, was on the sidelines, sipping his vodka and tonic. He liked to people watch and was taking in the party scene when he noticed Tyler staring so intensely across the room. At first, he wondered as to what or whom Tyler was looking so intently.

Oh, my God, thought Christopher. *He's staring at Ben Thompson.*

Christopher didn't know Tyler personally. He had seen him in the last comedy, *Out of Order,* a farce that the community theater had presented. Tyler was hysterically funny in the second leading role. Christopher did know that Tyler was the gay florist in town. Gay or not, he was very convincing playing a heterosexual in that play.

Christopher watched Tyler watch Ben kiss Jacqueline, and he saw Tyler blink back the tears. Although Christopher didn't like seeing anyone in pain, it wasn't his style to intervene in something as personal as this matter appeared. He would just walk away. For some odd reason, this time he didn't. Summoning all the courage he could muster, he walked quietly up to Tyler and gently placed his hand on Tyler's shoulder. In a voice that only Tyler could hear, Christopher said, "Please forgive me. I know you don't know me, and I really don't mean to intrude, but I'm compelled to tell you two things. One, no one can help who he falls in love with, and, two, he is so not worth it, buddy." With that, Christopher walked away.

Tyler, stunned by what the handsome stranger said to him, watched Christopher as he disappeared into the crowd. It was time to leave. He pulled himself together and went to find Magda and Sophie.

CHAPTER NINE

A week after Labor Day, Tyler was putting out additional fall decorations and merchandise at Tyler's Floral and Gifts. Autumn was rapidly approaching with the maple tree outside the store trading its greenery for reds, yellows and orange. He was unpacking the Halloween items: witches, pumpkins, gourds, and black cats. Tyler was especially fond of the ceramic pumpkin teapots that he had ordered from his supplier.

Sophie was in the back room putting up an order for a funeral that had just been phoned in. In walked Christopher Girrardi and his wife, Karen. Tyler recognized them from Armella's party and couldn't help but remember Christopher's words to him.

"How may I help you?" Tyler asked.

Karen retorted, "We're just looking. I've heard a lot about you and your shop."

"All good, I hope. I'm Tyler. If you have any questions, please ask. Feel free to look around."

Christopher smiled and said, "Thanks. We will."

Tyler continued working on the Halloween display, very much aware that Christopher was looking at him intently while his wife just browsed. He was thinking that of the two, Christopher was definitely more interesting and friendlier.

Karen spoke to her husband. "Let's go, Chris. I don't see anything here that I want."

"Whatever you say." He appeared to be resigned to be with her and was just along for the ride, indulging her whims on this excursion of theirs. Karen Girrardi exited the store without saying a word.

"Thank you. Have a good day," Tyler said as the door shut.

Christopher turned his head, "You, too. Thank you."

Sophie walked up to the counter from the back room just in time to catch their departure. "They didn't buy anything?"

"No. Apparently she didn't like anything she saw here." "They were at Carmella's party."

"Yes, I remember." Tyler also remembered that he hadn't told Sophie or Magda about Christopher's comments to him that evening regarding Ben.

"I heard that they have a fabulous big house in Ludington. They're very well-off. His family has money, and she probably married him for it."

Tyler quipped, "If you can't be with someone for love, then you might as well be with them for money."

"You don't really believe that, Tyler Reynolds, and you know it."

Tyler was deep in thought. There was something about Christopher today that struck him. He was polite but seemed like a fish out of water with his wife while the two of them were in the shop browsing. *I'm sure he was bored. He'd probably rather be outside throwing a football with his buds. Christopher was very masculine, a man's man. Yet, he also had a sensitive side that he allowed me to see. That's a very attractive combination of character traits. After all, he did venture forth and say what he did to me at Carmella's party. That was very perceptive of him.* Tyler smiled at the recollection of Christopher offering his words of solace during a somber moment that no one else had seemed to witness. When he thought about it later, he was extremely flattered that a total stranger would actually have that kind of courage.

"Sophie, I think those two are the classic case of the cheerleader marrying the captain of the football team." Tyler had no idea of how accurate his assessment of Christopher and Karen Girrardi was.

The following Saturday morning, Tyler was sitting on the log at the beach of Lake Michigan, meditating. He loved to come here before it got busy with others walking the beach. His spot was about a hundred feet from the water's edge. The peace he felt here in God's world was always a great comfort. He closed his eyes, and the sound of the water took him out to that inner temple where he could listen to what Spirit had to say. Sometimes he didn't "hear" anything. That was okay, too. He felt as though the peace of the Divine filled his body. It was as if it entered through the top of his head and filled every cell in his being. He let it pour in for twenty or thirty minutes. It re-charged him for the day. He felt like he could handle anything life brought his way.

Tyler came back to the real world from his meditation as he heard footsteps in the sand approaching him. It was Christopher Girrardi, attired in his navy blue running suit and obviously out jogging that morning.

"Good morning, Tyler."

"Hi."

"I'm not imposing on your space, am I?"

"No, I just finished meditating. It's all good."

Extending his right hand toward Tyler, "Christopher Girrardi. We haven't really formally met. I just wanted to say hello. I was in your floral shop last week with my wife."

Shaking Christopher's hand firmly, "Christopher. Yes you were, and you also spoke to me at Carmella's party."

"About that. Listen, I was way out of line to do that, and I want to apologize. I had no right to say what I did. That's not my nature to intrude on a private moment like that."

"Ah, but you did."

"I happened to observe you watching Reverend Ben Thompson, andI felt so compelled to say something. Anyway, I was out of line for speaking, and I am really sorry."

"Mr. Girrardi, I accept your apology. But you were very accurate in your assessment of that moment."

"Please, call me Christopher. Mister makes me sound old. Chris is good, too."

"I'll call you Christopher. I like using one's full name. I find the sound of it aesthetically pleasing. As for the sounding old stuff, age is just a number. With all due respect, sir, I'm guessing that you are only a few years older than I am."

"Not that much, I'm sure."

"A little older, perhaps, and a little wiser. I wasn't aware that I was wearing my heart on my sleeve at that moment at Carmella's party. Perhaps, I owe you an apology for allowing you to see that. Thinking back to your actions towards me then, I thought it was rather brave and very gallant', (with the stress on the last syllable) debonair, and kind." Affecting a southern accent, "I have always relied on the kindness of strangers."

"What?"

"Never mind. That was a very bad delivery of a Blanche Dubois line from *A Streetcar Named Desire*. Thanks for stopping to say hello. I need to go home and get ready for work, and you need to finish jogging. Have a nice weekend."

"You too, Tyler."

As Tyler walked to his car he turned and watched Christopher jog along the water's edge until he was out of sight. *What a nice man!*

CHAPTER TEN

The following Wednesday Tyler was swamped at the floral shop. Business was brisk, so he wasn't complaining, but Sophie had taken the morning off to go with Magda to the hospital to have tests done. Magda was usually calm and collected about anything that came her way, but she wasn't this time. She wouldn't say what the CAT scan and other tests were for, but Tyler and Sophie insisted that one of them would go with her. Sophie and Tyler were the only "family" she had. Tyler had sent Magda some absentee healing earlier before he started in on the orders needing to be filled. The phone had been ringing constantly with new orders, so he had put the phone on speaker so he could work on arrangements while talking until he had to stop and write down what the customer wanted.

Tyler realized that he was getting seriously behind without Sophie there. "My Angels, help me get everything done on a timely basis today, and may it all be the best work that I have ever done. Thank you for your help."

Five minutes later, Christopher walked into the floral shop.

"Hey, Tyler."

"Hi, Christopher, what can I do for you today?"

"You look like you're really busy."

"I am. My assistant, Sophie, isn't here now. She's with our friend at the hospital. How can I help you?"

"I'm sorry to bother you at work, but I didn't see a home phone number listed in the book, so I couldn't call you."

"That would be because I no longer have a landline at home. I only have my cell phone. Why did you need to call me?"

"Because this is a personal matter, not business."

Tyler felt his body stiffen as he straightened up, chest out. Taking a deep breath as if bracing for bad news, "Oh?" "I was wondering if you would have lunch with me sometime."

"Lunch? Really? Why? Thanks, but I make it a rule to not socialize with my customers."

Smiling and using all of his charm, Christopher stated, "Then I'm in luck. I haven't ever purchased anything from you, so technically I'm not a customer."

"Thanks, but no thank you. My assistant is not here. Even if she was, we seldom take a lunch break. We kind of snack when we can. I do appreciate the gesture. It was nice of you to ask."

"Okay. Perhaps another time."

Tyler smiled and sort of shook his head "no" as Christopher left the store. Interesting. *Why did this very married, very manly heterosexual want to have lunch?* He quickly decided that he really didn't have the time to ponder why.

Christopher thought hard. That night at Carmella's party when he first saw Tyler, an old "stirring" deep within had been re-awakened. He had put those feelings away during his college days. They were put away for good. Honestly, he had never thought about forging that kind of deep relationship with another man since then. He was happy with his career. His marriage was okay, not great. He accepted that fact as well. Then he saw Tyler.

Unexplicably, Christopher realized that he needed a male friend that he could trust telling anything. His gut instinct told him to befriend Tyler. For now he would trust that intuition.

He wanted to know Tyler better and wouldn't take "no" for an answer. He was determined to have lunch with Tyler. Christopher admired Tyler's spunk. He was just who he was, take it or leave it. Christopher found that honesty refreshing. How many times could he hope to catch Tyler at the beach meditating and just run into him and try to make conversation? Christopher knew that if he could just somehow break the ice with Tyler, that they would have a connection. How was he going to make it happen?

Christopher glanced at his watch--11:30 a.m. The deli across the street was starting to get busy. Impulsively, he crossed the street, entered the door, and went up to the counter. The clerk was just finishing up with the customer ahead of him. When it was his turn, he ordered two sandwiches to go. What looked good? He opted for the black forest ham on rye, spicy mustard, lettuce, onion, and a roasted turkey on whole wheat, light mayo, lettuce, tomato, a regular bottle of water, and a bottle of sparkling water.

Tyler was concerned that he had heard nothing from Sophie. Neither of them had any idea how long it would take at the hospital with Magda. Even when they were through, it was an hour's drive home. No call or text yet; she should have communicated via his cell phone by now. *Well, no news is good news.*

There were orders that needed to be delivered. Tyler needed to order more flowers and supplies. In the old days, he would have succumbed to being overwhelmed and started to panic. Today, there wasn't time.

Christopher walked back into the shop with lunch in hand.
"Hello, again. What's up?"
"Relax, my friend. Look, you're swamped. You need some help. You need to eat some real food, not junk food," he said as he opened up the sandwiches, giving each one of them a half. "I'm

pretty sure that you can eat either ham or turkey or both. And although you look like you could use a good stiff drink right now, you had better stick with water. I have the day off. Let me help you."

"Well, I…" Tyler was at a loss for words.

"I don't know anything about arranging flowers, but I can answer the phone. I can make deliveries for you. I know how to operate a cash register. I used to work in retail while I was going to college."

"I don't know you that well. I can't ask you to do that."

"You don't have to ask me. I offered, and wouldn't it be fun to get to know each other?"

"I don't know. Would it?"

The phone rang, and Christopher grabbed it before Tyler could.

"Tyler"s Floral and Gifts. How may I help you?"

Christopher grabbed a pen and started writing fast and furiously.

"Yes. Yes. We can do that. And the price range? $90 to a $100? Of course. Where would you like that delivered to? Today after 4:00? On your account here? Certainly." He looked at Tyler for approval.

Tyler nodded, "Yes, sure." Then he muttered under his breath, "What the hell!"

"That wasn't so hard. It was kind of fun."

"Oh, we have a hell of a good time here," Tyler said with a tinge of sarcasm.

"You know, if you keep working while I answer the phone, you can get caught up."

"Who made you my boss?"

"Sorry. I'm used to delegating. You're still the boss."

"Thank you. Besides, that time I had to listen. Quality control, I think it's called in the rest of the world."

The phone stopped ringing. They ate their sandwiches while Tyler kept working. When a customer entered the store, Christopher waited on them. He would ask Tyler if he had a question about something.

When the store was free of customers, Tyler asked, "So, do you do this kind of volunteer work often? Because I can't afford to pay you. At least not much. Why are you helping me? Why do you want to have lunch with me anyway?"

"You seem like a nice guy. I'm a nice guy. Frankly, I don't have any close friends."

"Really? Not anyone you work out with or socialize with? No close buds that you can pour your heart out to?"

"No, I don't. There you have it. I've put all of my cards on the table. I'm making the first gesture. Whether we actually become good friends or not, remains to be seen. But I thought I'd make the first move."

Maybe, Tyler thought, his mind racing as to what kind of friendship this oh-so-married, masculine, and incredibly handsome man wanted from him. "I guess we'll see how that unfolds."

The afternoon passed quickly. Christopher was in the front of the shop running the cash register for customers who came in to purchase items. Tyler worked frantically and consequently stayed on top of things. Around 2:30 he sent Christopher out with the van to make deliveries. He'd had a text from Sophie. The doctors wanted to run more tests on Magda in the afternoon, so she wouldn't be in today. "How are things at the store?"

Tyler sent a text back that he was managing, not to worry, and just be with Magda and to hug her for him. He'd tell her about Christopher tomorrow. To be honest, he was very grateful for Christopher's help. *Why was he doing this? Suddenly, he wants us to be best buds? It doesn't matter.* Tyler had invoked his angels for help to get through the day, and Christopher showed up. "Don't look a gift horse in the mouth," his mother would have said. Funny that he thought about her now in the midst of the day. *I wonder how she is doing? I'm sure that she's fine.* Tyler dismissed any further thoughts of the mother he hadn't seen or communicated with in almost fourteen years. Why should he? When he was sixteen, she asked him if it was true that he was gay. He told her yes. She told him if that was the case that he had two hours to get out and that she never wanted to see him again. And, so he left. That was a lot of tears ago. Tyler had moved on.

When Christopher returned from making the deliveries, he put a handful of dollar bills down on the counter.

"What's that for?" Tyler asked.

"Tips I received today. I told them all it wasn't necessary, but some of the customers insisted."

"It's yours. Keep it. I promise I won't tell the IRS if you decide not to declare it. Take this bouquet of flowers home to your wife for your day's work."

"I would but she's not there. We're separated."

"Oh?"

Reading Tyler's face, Christopher elaborated. "It's a trial separation. We'll see if we can reconcile irreconcilable differences."

"Sorry to hear that. I didn't know. Then the flowers are for you."

"I really enjoyed helping you out today. Thank you."

"No, thank you! I desperately need help today so I asked the angels, and you showed up. Just like that. Now, you can add this life-altering experience to your resume."

"I'll do that. Do you have plans for this evening? Maybe we could have dinner?"

"I have a rehearsal for a play I'm in. Community theater at its best. We open in two weeks. It's a comedy, See How They Run. You should come see it."

"I will. Perhaps another time we can have dinner then."

"Perhaps. Time to lock up. Thanks again for your help, Christopher. You were a life-saver today. You get a merit badge."

"Okay, see you soon." With that remark, Christopher left.

God, he's a lonely man, I guess. Sad, because he has so much to offer. Tyler shrugged his shoulders and started to look over his script in preparation for the evening's rehearsal.

Friday evening of the following week, Tyler agreed to meet Christopher for dinner at Ruth's Chris in Grand Rapids. Secretly, Tyler had been curious to dine here, but it was a bit of drive from Pentwater and somewhat pricey. Tyler just figured dining here would have to wait for a special occasion for he and his friends to justify. He told Christopher he would meet him at the restaurant at 7:00 p.m. No, Christopher couldn't pick him up. That would be like a date in Tyler's mind, and he wasn't going to do that with this prominently married man, separated or not. Besides, it was always good to have one's own transportation in case one wanted to make a fast exit.

Tyler had worn his navy blue vest over a white patterned shirt with khaki pants. He wanted to look casual but not too conservative-looking for this restaurant. He did look good in this ensemble, he had to admit.

Tyler arrived promptly at 7:00 and told the maitre d' that he was to join a Mr. Christopher Girrardi. "Right this way, sir. "

Tyler was impressed with the décor of the restaurant. There was lots of cherry wood, brass, and glass. Multi-colored freesias filled the vases on each table. The waiters and waitresses were impeccably attired in white shirts, black slacks, and black vests. They all appeared confident that they would give the customers an unforgettable dining experience.

Christopher was sitting in a corner booth drinking red wine; the newly-opened bottle was on the table. Clad in a sport coat, open collar shirt and dress slacks, he stood and beamed when Tyler walked in. "I took the liberty of ordering some wine. If you would like something else, please say so."

Smiling back at him, "Wine is perfect." Tyler avoided liquor. Two cocktails and he got brutally honest with people, whether they liked it or not. He really didn't like the way his body felt after drinking liquor, so he avoided it.

The waiter pushed in Tyler's chair and filled Tyler's wine glass. "Would you gentlemen care for an appetizer?"

"You order. What's good, Christopher?"

"We'll start with an order of the calamari and some bruschetta, please."

"An excellent choice, sir," as the waiter left their table.

"I like both. This is a very nice place, classy but not piss elegant."

If nothing else happened this evening, Tyler was curious to find out what Christopher wanted in the way of friendship. It was sad not to have someone one could confide in. Not that Tyler wasn't up to the task, but he also wasn't looking to be someone's therapist either. As Sophie had told him, "Have dinner with him. Enjoy the evening. Have fun, for once."

Raising his glass in a toast, "So, Christopher, here we are."

"Here we are."

A little nervous, Christopher started the conversation. He somehow segued from the drive over to talking about his childhood, his love of sports, especially football, his work. He ran the marketing company that his father had started.

"So what's your title? CEO?"

"Yes. I just think that sometimes it sounds pretentious to say that when I'm getting to know someone."

"I don't find you to be pretentious at all."

To Tyler's self-surprise, he found the man fascinating. He was opening up to a relative stranger. Christopher seemed starved for someone to just listen to him. After awhile, he stopped, "I must be boring you. I've been doing all of the talking."

"You're not boring me at all. You've had a rather interesting life." Here was this ruggedly handsome, 6'2" chestnut-haired man with the football player's build who could be out with anyone, spending his Friday evening with me, hungry for someone to listen to him. *He's so lonely,* thought Tyler. *He must not have any close friends, which I find strange.*

"Your turn," Christopher encouraged Tyler as he refilled their wine glasses.

"My life doesn't read as well as yours I'm afraid. Although you willingly shared your growing-up experiences, I can't share mine. I won't. A lot of it was too painful. One plays the cards one is dealt. I moved on. I like being a florist. My business is successful. I love the theater and old movies. I do volunteer work in community theater, onstage and backstage in my spare time, and I'm openly gay."

"I know you are."

"Let's cut to the chase, Christopher. What is all of this about? What do you want from me? We're not in the same social circles. We're certainly not in the same financial bracket. You're straight, and I'm gay."

"Don't you have any straight friends?"

"Yes."

Christopher paused a moment as if trying to find the correct words. "I have never told anyone this, but I feel I can tell you. I'm a pretty shrewd observer of people, and I have this gut instinct that I can trust you."

"I'll take that as a compliment. I don't betray confidences."

"I'm hoping you don't. I need a really good friend, Tyler. I don't want to burden you with a responsibility you haven't asked for."

"What is it, Christopher?"

"I have these feelings again. Maybe I'm not so straight after all. I haven't thought about being with a man since college. Never had the desire again until that night I saw you at Carmella's party and it all came flooding back to me."

Tyler took a deep breath. "Let me try to understand this. You saw me crying over Ben Thompson and that made you think that you want to be with a man sexually?"

Christopher fumbled for words and was clutching his wine glass tightly. "Yes. Maybe. I don't know. I guess so."

"Is this why you and your wife separated?"

"Not really. It wasn't a good marriage for lots of reasons that I don't want to go into now. I did lose interest in her sexually but it wasn't because I was thinking about men."

"Okay."

"Maybe I'm bisexual."

"Maybe. I don't know what to think about those who claim to be bi. I have never had a desire to be straight. I knew who I was and 'straight' wasn't me. There was a time in my younger days when if someone asked me 'What is your definition of a bi-sexual?' I would have said a bisexual is someone who can't make a decision. Now, I'm not so sure. You can have two points, one on each end of the spectrum. One point is exclusively heterosexual, and the other end is exclusively homosexual, and you have all of these degrees of variance, what one will or won't do with the same gender in between. In the very center is a point that we will call bi-sexual. I suppose that a bi-sexual is someone who feels totally comfortable having sex with either same or opposite genders. In my opinion, one's head is always in a certain place regardless of the gender that he happens to be with at the moment. O, God, listen to me. 'Off and running!' Sorry."

"It does make sense, though."

"Have you ever thought of being with another woman, Christopher? Either during your marriage or now?"

"No, I haven't." There was an awkward silence. "Tyler, would you be willing to help me explore this, to see if I am really bi-sexual or gay or just a straight man with abnormal feelings?"

"I don't think it is abnormal to be with a man."

"Sorry. Poor choice of words."

"Forget it."

"Tyler, I'm not very good with this." Christopher paused, then blurted out, "Would you go to bed with me?"

Although incensed, Tyler retained his composure. He didn't raise his voice. He clenched his right hand on the edge of his chair. No one could see his white knuckles squeezing the chair. Looking directly at Christopher and speaking very deliberately so only Christopher could hear him, "I see. The gay guy with all of the experience can just jump into bed with the handsome married man, so he can do whatever he wants to do, so that he can figure out his life, satisfy his urges and move on with his life."

"It's not like that. I like you. I don't want it to be with just anybody."

"I guess I'm supposed to feel flattered that you chose me. But I don't. I feel great sadness. You're an incredibly handsome man, Christopher Girrardi. Lots of people would jump at the chance to go to bed with you. But if I'm supposed to feel flattered that you picked me, I'm not. I'm not interested. Just because I'm gay you thought I would just jump at the chance to go to bed with a stud like you? Like you're doing me some kind of favor? Let me throw the jilted gay guy a bone?"

"No, I didn't mean it like that. I—"

Tyler cut Christopher off. "I am so goddam tired, knowingly or unknowingly, of helping people figure out who the fuck they are. It's exhausting, and I still end up alone."

"But Tyler…"

Tyler was on a roll. A lot of anger came bubbling out. "You should have just asked me upfront, and I would have told you no.

Saved you the price of a dinner and a wasted Friday night for both of us." He pulled out a fifty dollar bill from his wallet and put it on the table. "Put this towards my share of dinner. Christopher, guys like you are a dime a dozen. Most of the gay or bi men I meet are married. They just want someone like me waiting for them on the sidelines whenever they get the urge to fool around. They stay married so everyone else in town will continue to think that they are fine, upstanding men, pillars of society. Those same people think that someone like me is a nothing because he is alone. At least I know who I am! I just had a man who I loved dearly leave me for a woman. I don't need someone who is already married."

"I know Ben hurt you. I'm sorry. But I also told you that I'm separated."

"You're still married. Even if you divorce her, you'll marry some other woman. Why? Because you're weak. You were raised to be a heterosexual married man."

"Please don't do this. I'm trying to deal with it."

"I don't get involved with married men because the bottom line is I KNOW who you will be with on New Year's Eve, and it isn't me. I'm not interested in being your experiment, your fuck buddy, your friend with benefits, or whatever name you want to give it. I'm not playing this game with you or with anyone."

"Tyler, please."

"Please what? Find yourself a good therapist. Then go online and find yourself a cute call boy. One can find anything online. Go to a big city, Chicago or New York, and play out of town. Figure it out there."

Tyler got up to leave. "For some stupid reason unbeknownst to me, I had the incredibly dumb idea that maybe you liked me for me and not what I could do for you. Stupid, stupid me." Much more disappointed than he realized, Tyler turned and left the restaurant, blinking back the tears. What he didn't see were the tears in Christopher's eyes. No one did. He turned away as he downed the remaining wine in his glass. Leaving much more than enough money to cover the bill, Christopher walked out of the restaurant hoping no one could see how awful he felt inside.

CHAPTER ELEVEN

The weeks flew by since that Friday evening dinner with Christopher. When Sophie had asked him how it went, he replied, "I only had an appetizer. He wanted something from me that I can't give. There's nothing more to say." Sophie knew Tyler well enough to know that his response really had a lot more behind it. However, she would respect his right to not go into detail. It had been a spectacularly lovely autumn in Michigan that year. Tyler often commented to himself enroute to work on the majesty all of the trees' blazing hues blending together. Halloween came and went. Tyler always thought it interesting that when people were in costume, they let their masks down. Next year, he would have to plan and host a costume party.

Work was busy, and Tyler was grateful. Thanksgiving closed out November with the best month so far of the year. Magda and Sophie were at Tyler's for Thanksgiving dinner. This was Tyler's favorite dinner of the year to prepare. He loved to cook for people he loved. Maybe, he thought, *If I ever get tired of the flower business, I'll become a chef.*" Although he said he would take care of everything,

Magda did bring her sweet potato pie to everyone's delight. The three were also celebrating that Magda's issue (she refused to give it energy by mentioning the cancer) that had been discovered months earlier, was in remission. They all had much to be grateful for.

Christmas always made December a very busy month. Tyler spent much more time decorating the shop than he did at home this year. That was work. However, at home, he only put up a small tree just so he could say he had one. His heart wasn't in it this year. Last Christmas he thought surely he would be celebrating with Ben. How long did Ben have to be married before he realized that it was Tyler that he needed to be with? At least that's what Tyler told himself whenever he thought about Ben, which was often. *How much longer of living a lie before Ben realized that Tyler really did know what was best for him?* They were soul mates, and one day Ben would come to his senses. How could he not?

How did Tyler know that he and Ben were soul mates? Soon after Tyler and Ben started seeing each other, Tyler decided he wanted to experience a past life regression. Magda referred him to a friend of hers who specialized in them. Her name was Sally, and she lived in a small house in the woods near a lake. "How did you find me?" Sally asked when Tyler contacted her. "I don't advertise."

"My friend Magda referred me."

"Then you are meant to be here."

Sally explained what would happen in the regression. Tyler would recline on the chaise lounge with his eyes closed. He would be aware of the noises of the house and the birds chirping in the woods outside. Sally would talk him down back into time, starting with one hundred. He would always be safe. He could ask her questions at any time. If at any time he felt uncomfortable, just say so, and Sally would end the session. She told him that perhaps nothing would happen for him. This was often common for many with their first regression. "Just be open."

Tyler closed his eyes. Sally started with a prayer, asking the Divine to be with Tyler to show him in a loving and gentle way anything that he needed to know as it related to his current lifetime.

"One hundred, ninety-nine, ninety-eight, ninety-seven. You are deeply relaxed." She guided him through the relaxation of every muscle from his neck down to his toes. Every so often, Sally threw in some more numbers as she counted downwards, continually reminding Tyler of how relaxed he was. Tyler was being a good sport about it but thought that it wasn't working. He didn't really think that he was all that relaxed. He wanted to experience "something." *Relax or you won't see or feel anything.* He clearly heard the cuckoo clock chime 2:00 p.m. Finally, Sally had Tyler walk down a long winding staircase. At the foot of the stairs were three doors, which he very clearly saw. "Choose a door. Open it, and step through. What do you see?"

Tyler did as Sally asked. He opened a door and stepped over the threshold.

"I'm in ancient Egypt. I see pyramids in the near distance."

"Are you helping to build the pyramids?"

"No, I'm a slave in the Pharaoh's household. I primarily serve one of the Pharoh's main advisors."

"Is this advisor your boss??

"Yes."

"Do you see him?"

"Yes. It's Ben!"

Tyler told Sally the details of what he saw. It was like watching and being in a movie all at the same time. He had loved Ben in that lifetime as well. It was a mutual love that went unspoken. He was never mistreated by Ben in that role. A huge flood was coming and many would perish if they remained. At the end of his life, Ben gave Tyler his freedom, but Tyler didn't want to leave his master. The tidal wave of water came and Tyler watched his body being pulled from Ben's grasp. He drowned and just floated away with the other debris.

Sally thought it best to bring Tyler back to the present at that time. The regression certainly answered many questions about his current relationship. When he came out of it, Tyler realized what a valuable tool a past life regression could be in understanding current situations.

In the meantime, Tyler had been asked to serve as property master for the community theater production of *Guys and Dolls."* He had had opportunities to date, but always said, "No, thanks. I'm not dating now." The director, Jim Paxton, finally said, "Well, then how about just sex? Skip the dating part, Tyler."

"Thanks, Jim. But let's just create good theater together and leave it at that."

"So do you go to bars? Where do you go to get laid?"

"What I'm looking for isn't in a bar. I'm going through a period of self-imposed celibacy. But thanks for the offer."

One Sunday afternoon that fall, Tyler was perusing the paper when he noticed the picture of the "Pet of the Week." She was a cocker spaniel mix that needed a good home. Tyler was at the animal shelter the next morning when they opened. When he and the dog saw each other, it was love at first sight. "You look like a 'Sadie.'" Tyler paid for her shots and neutering procedure and Sadie came home with him the next day. She appeared to be about two years-old and only took about a day to get house-broken. It was more a matter of just getting used to Tyler's house than anything. Sadie was great company. Between taking care of her and working in the theater in the evening, Tyler had no time to think about dating and he was okay with that.

"So what are you doing for New Year's Eve this year, Tyler?" Sophie inquired that morning of. The shop would close at noon, and they were both glad for a long weekend off.

"I was invited to a party at Michael's, but I already gave them my regrets. I'd rather stay home tonight. I'm going to fix a very nice dinner for Sadie and myself. Build a fire in the fireplace, open a bottle of wine, read from a good book, then go to bed early. When I wake up, it will be next year, a time for new beginnings. New Year's Eve is highly over-rated.

"Why don't you come over to Magda's? We're going to hang out, play games, give each other readings. It will be fun, just the three of us."

"I told her that I would stop over tomorrow afternoon. Besides, we're supposed to get a bad snow storm tonight, so it's a good night to stay home. I really don't want to be out on the road with all of the drunks anyway."

Sadie was eagerly awaiting Tyler when he got home. "Did you miss me, sweetness? Yes, I missed you too. He gave her a treat, and she was happy. *Who needs a man?* Tyler thought. *An affectionate dog gives me all of the company and unconditional love I need.* With that, Tyler put a pork roast in the oven, took down the Christmas tree, put away the ornaments, and finished making dinner.

By 7:00 p.m. it was snowing hard. He opened a bottle of merlot. By 9:00 he had finished eating, cleared the table, and put two more logs on the fire. He settled down with a cup of coffee, a snifter with some Amaretto, and Sadie on his right side of the sofa. Staring into the fire, he was lost in thought. *Well, this is where you are today, Tyler Reynolds. Where are you headed with this new year? Are you going to keep on waiting for Ben to get his shit together? Or are you going to be able to truly let him go and move on?"* If only his brain could convince his heart, this would all be so much easier. Tyler must have dozed off as he was awakened not by the clock chiming 11:00 p.m., but by Sadie's bark and the hair standing up on the scruff of her neck.

"What is it Sadie?" She had only been with Tyler for two months but she "owned" her new territory. Sadie jumped up off of the sofa and went toward the front door. She stood there and growled. "What is it, Sadie?" Then came the knocking on the door, followed by the ringing of the doorbell.

"Okay, okay. I'm coming."

Tyler got up to open the door with Sadie, his protector, in front of him.

Upon opening the door, there stood Christopher, covered in snow, grinning, and holding a bottle of champagne in one hand. "It's New Year's Eve, Tyler, and I know who I want to be with," he blurted out, the smell of alcohol on his person.

"What the fuck! I hope you're not driving."

"I'm not drunk. I'm just happy."

"Yes, you are!"

"No, I'm not driving. I left that dive bar downtown because they wouldn't serve me anymore. It's snowing a lot, you know, and I ended up in a snow bank about a mile from here. So here I am. Want a drink? Let's bring in the New Year together."

"Christopher! You walked a mile in this storm? Do you have your keys? I'll take you home."

"Please, let me stay here. It's New Year's Eve."

"I know."

"I don't want to go home. I don't want to be alone."

"Oh, Christ. I suppose. Well, come inside and get warmed up. You can't be out in this weather."

"Thanks." Christopher put his keys into Tyler's hand. "Hang on to these for me, please."

"Your shoes and socks are soaked. So are your pants."

"I told you it's snowing outside, heavy, wet snow."

"I can see that. Take those wet clothes off here. I don't want you tracking all through my house. I'll get you some dry socks and sweats to put on. Sadie, you keep your eye on him.

Tyler returned with a bath towel, socks, sweat pants, and an extra large sweat shirt that he never wore. There stood Christopher stripped down to a tee shirt and his boxer briefs. Pretending not to notice, Tyler said, "Here, put these on. I think that they will fit. Give me your wet clothes so I can put them in the dryer."

When Tyler returned, Christopher was dressed in Tyler's clothes and was seated on the sofa facing the fire. "This is nice. Thanks. Let's open the champagne."

"I've got some coffee brewing. It will be ready in a few minutes."

"And ruin a good buzz?"

Tyler gave him a look that said, "I'm doing you a favor here."

"I suppose you're right."

"So where's your wife? Did you leave her in a snow bank?"

"No. I did not. I would never do that."

"I'm sorry. That remark was uncalled for."

"I have no idea where she is tonight. We're separated. I told you that last fall during the night of our ill-fated dinner. I'm going to file for divorce next week when my attorney gets back."

"Oh. You weren't able to work things out after how long together?"

"No. Five years. Long enough.

"Okay. So you're newly-single and went out tonight to get drunk, celebrate, whatever, and you drove off of the road into a ditch. Where is your cell phone? Why didn't you call road service for help?"

"Because I have been drinking and didn't want to risk having them call the cops. I didn't have your number, and I was on my way to see you."

"Me? Why?"

"Dinner didn't go well with us. At least I didn't do a very good job of telling you why I invited you out to dinner. You left angry, which I understand from your perspective. At least, I think I do. But I admire you. I respect you. I want to get to know you better. I find you incredibly attractive. Yes, I want to go to bed with you. I wouldn't be totally honest with you if I said I didn't. But please, Tyler, just give me a chance. Get to know me. I'm not a jerk. At least I try not to be."

Tyler turned his gaze away from Christopher and stared into the fire.

"Tyler, this is not the booze talking. It's me, the real authentic me, talking."

Authentic. How many times had Tyler used that word wishing Ben would come out of his closet?

For the first time in a long time, Tyler felt something stir inside. *What's that? And why now?* Was it compassion for this lonely man?

"I don't know what to say. You can stay here on the sofa tonight. I mean, you can't leave now. You're in no condition, and the weather isn't fit for man nor beast. Besides, your shoes are still wet. Why didn't you wear boots anyway?"

"They're not cool."

Tyler rolled his eyes. "I bet you were always one of the 'cool kids' at school weren't you?"

"I guess so. I don't know."

"In this weather, boots are practical. What do you think, Sadie? Can Christopher stay here tonight?" With that, Sadie went over and sniffed Christopher, and lay down at his feet.

"You're not helping any, Sadie." To Christopher, "Sadie says you can stay."

Smiling, "Thank you, Sadie. And thank you, Tyler. It's almost midnight. Can you turn on the TV so we can watch the ball drop in Times Square? We can open the champagne I brought and have a toast."

"All right, I suppose." Tyler handed the remote to Christopher. I'll get glasses." Tyler returned with the champagne glasses, Christopher had the TV on the appropriate channel and the bottle of champagne opened. He poured some into each glass as Tyler held them. Christopher set the bottle down as the countdown on the television began. "Nine, eight, seven, six, five, four, three, two, one. Happy New Year!" Auld Lang Syne began playing on the television as those in Times Square began screaming and cheering, hugging and kissing each other. Tyler and Christopher clinked glasses and toasted each other. "To a new year," said Tyler.

"To a new year and a new friendship," Christopher replied.

"To a new friendship."

Tyler downed his champagne. "I've never been much for champagne, but this is really good!"

"I'm glad you like it. Have some more," as he re-filled their glasses. Christopher sipped his and felt the best inside that he had felt in a LONG time.

"It's warm and cozy here."

"It is, Christopher. Thank you for the compliment."

After finishing the champagne, Tyler said, "It's been a long day. I'll get you a blanket and pillow."

"It's been a long year."

"It certainly has."

Tyler returned with two blankets and a couple of pillows. "The sofa isn't bad, and these should keep you warm enough. I turn the thermostat down at night to save on the heating bill."

"I'll be fine. Thanks, Tyler."

"Come on Sadie, bed time." Tyler went into his bedroom and shut the door, something he had never done since he had lived here. Stripped down to his underwear, he turned on the electric blanket and crawled under the covers of the queen-sized bed. Sadie was curled up at the foot. Tyler thought about the handsome man sleeping on his sofa in the next room. *What a way to end the year. What a way to start the new one.* Soon, they were both snoring away.

Tyler was up early the next day. He had let Sadie out to do her morning business and couldn't get back to sleep. He did a load of laundry and threw in Christopher's tee shirt, socks, and sport shirt in the same load. Christopher was still sound asleep on the sofa. Tyler was on his second cup of coffee. He decided to go outside and run the snow blower. He'd have to clear out the driveway anyway to get his car out. Later, they would have to go get Christopher's car out of the ditch if it hadn't been towed away.

When Tyler got back inside the house, Christopher was up drinking coffee. "I helped myself. Hope you don't mind."

"Not at all. How are you feeling?"

"Okay, no hangover."

"Good. Why don't you take a shower while I cook breakfast. I washed and dried your clothes so you would have something clean to put on.'

"What time did you get up?"

"Early, around 6:00. I'll nap later. After breakfast, we'll get your car, and then you can be on your way."

Tyler looked in his refrigerator to see what he could come up with for breakfast that was easy. "Ah, I know what I will concoct." He took a bag of hash brown potatoes out of the freezer and thawed them in the microwave. Then he diced onion and green pepper and sautéed them while he chopped the ham. He cracked a half dozen eggs open and beat them briefly, then added milk. He mixed all the ingredients together with the potatoes, added a can of mushrooms, poured it into a pan and covered it with shredded cheddar cheese and put the mixture in the oven to bake. "I think this will taste quite good." *Who are you trying to impress anyway, Tyler? No one,* he told himself. *It takes more than a baked Denver Omelet mixture to impress anyone.*

Christopher emerged from the bathroom showered and dressed and looked like a million bucks, even unshaven. Tyler found this day's growth of dark beard rather attractive.

"Be sure to take the toothbrush with you, compliments of my dental hygienist," Tyler offered.

Christopher wanted to say, "Can't I just leave it here to use next time?" but thought better of it and replied, "Okay, thanks."

As they sat down to breakfast, Christopher started the conversation where he had left off the previous evening. "I don't look at you as an experiment for me to find out if I'm really gay or not. I don't want to use you for that. I do want to get to know you better. Couldn't we do things together? Get to know each other? Talk to me about what it is like to live openly as a gay man, proud and tall."

Tyler paused a long time. "Okay, what the hell? Although I doubt that we have anything in common, we can see how that plays out. But I'm going to tell you right now that we will never have sex with each other. So if your ultimate goal is to bed me down so I can be a notch on your bedpost, that's not going to happen." Tyler looked away briefly, then returned to look Christopher directly in the eye. "It's not that you're not attractive, you have many fine qualities, kindness being a major one, and to speak frankly, having seen you in just your boxer briefs last night, you would be bringing a LOT to the table." He paused again, "I've been around the block a time or two, Christopher. I'm beyond going gaga over a handsome man with a big dick. Been there and done that. I believe in laying the cards on the table. Just an FYI."

"Okay, that's fair. And honest. Here's an FYI for you. I haven't been with anyone sexually since the last time I was with my wife."

"Okay. Duly noted. I haven't been with anyone since Ben." A beat. "Why are we telling each other this information when we are never going to have sex with each other?"

"It's all part of getting to know each other."

"Hmmm."

"What do you like to do? Where would you like to go on a date?"

"We might do things together, but it's not a date."

"Okay, we can just do things, go places together. Get to know each other."

"Okay. I like the theater, the symphony, a good movie. I don't like movies that are too real, where the violence is so believable. I don't like seeing one human being inflicting pain on another. I do like, and I hate this expression, chick flicks. I like working in my yard and getting my hands in the dirt. I like going to a decent bar, a gay bar, and going dancing. I would like to travel. I want to go to Italy one day, to Tuscany."

"It's beautiful there."

"You've been there?" Christopher nodded affirmatively. "I envy that. And you? What do you enjoy doing?"

"I also like the theater, the arts, and the symphony. I LOVE sports, watching and playing, especially football. Do you like sports?"

"I don't know anything about sports. I don't understand football. Baseball is tedious to watch. Golf is for rich people."

"You're being judgmental."

"Your point is well-taken. I was never any good at any sport. In gym class, I was the last kid chosen when we had to divide up in teams. No one wanted me on his team because I was so bad. It didn't matter what it was, flag football, basketball, volleyball. It didn't matter. Gym class was a nightmare. I hated it."

"Would you go with me to a pro football game?"

"Will you go with me to the opera?" Tyler hadn't ever been to the opera, but wanted to attend.

"Sure. That would be fair."

"Okay. For now, let's eat breakfast, and then we'll go see about your car."

"It smells good and I'm famished."

"Would you like whole wheat toast to go with your Denver omelet?"

Christopher smiled, "Thanks, that would be perfect." This New Year was starting out so much better than he had imagined. Tyler smiled as he watched Christopher enjoy breakfast.

After breakfast they ventured outside. The sun was shining on the white, cold landscape.

By some stroke of luck, Christopher's car was still in the snow bank on the side of the road. Tyler pushed and Christopher backed it right out into the road. Thankfully, it didn't take much effort.

"Thanks for everything," Christopher yelled as he drove off.

Damn, thought Tyler, *now I'll have to brush up on opera.*

CHAPTER TWELVE

And so Tyler began to "see" Christopher. Their first evening out was to a movie starring Bruce Willis, one of his action-filled films. It was similar to *Die Hard* only with a different title. Christopher let Tyler pick the film. Tyler chose this one because he thought he could get through it, and he thought that it might be one that Christopher would enjoy. When Tyler reached for his wallet to pay for his ticket, Christopher stopped him. "Put that away. I've got it covered."

"Then next time is on me."

Shit, what did you say that for, Tyler? he said to himself. *Now that means you have to go out with him again.*"

"Okay. Sure," was Christopher's reply.

When the film was over, Christopher gave his review. "Not a great movie, but it was entertaining."

"That's what I thought too," Tyler agreed as they walked toward Christopher's dark blue BMW with the rich grey leather interior.

As Christopher unlocked his vehicle, he asked, "The night's still young. Want to get a drink?"

"Yeah, that's a good idea."

Christopher took them to a small bistro that had an extensive wine collection.

Perusing the wine list, Christopher asked, "Red or white? Shall we order a bottle?"

"I guess it depends how thirsty you are. One glass is enough for me. I'll get the wine since you paid for the movie tickets."As the evening progressed, and the conversation deepened, Tyler found himself actually enjoying himself more than he had thought possible.

"So does anyone ever call you Chris?" inquired Tyler.

"It's about half and half. I was Chris growing up. My mother wanted to call me Christopher, but I told her I liked Chris instead."

"She probably only called you Christopher when you were in trouble."

"She did but that wasn't often. I was a good kid."

"I can call you Chris if you prefer. It's just that you introduced yourself as Christopher, not 'Chris'. Even if you hadn't, I tend to call people by their full name. Christopher has such an esthetically pleasing sound to it. It fits you."

"Anybody ever call you Ty?"

"Occasionally, Hank did after he got to know me. But he's the only one who ever did."

"Who's Hank?"

"A very nice man I lived with for a few years, sometime ago. He was like a dad to me. He rescued me when I had nowhere to turn."

Christopher leaned forward, keenly interested. "This was after you left home?"

"Yes. That's a story for another time. Hank taught me the flower business. Then he died."

"What happened?"

"Heart attack. Out of the blue. He went in his sleep, which certainly is a nice way to make one's transition. One minute he was there, the next minute he wasn't. But that's life, isn't it?"

"I'm sorry."

Shrugging his shoulders, "Thanks. What doesn't kill you, is supposed to give you character and make you stronger." Chuckling, Tyler added, "If that was really true, I would be able to bench press a Buick."

Christopher seemed quite taken and boldly asked, "Sooooo, do you think I could call you Ty?"

"Thanks for asking. Not yet." *At least he asked and just didn't assume. What a kind man.*

Christopher was intrigued with Tyler's past which was so unlike his. "Out of curiosity, if Hank hadn't died, do you think that you would still be with him, helping him with his business?"

Tyler had never thought of this. "I don't know. Probably. Life was good then. But that isn't how the cookie crumbled."

Changing the subject, Tyler asked, "I was an only child. How about you? Any siblings?"

"None that I know of. When I was eighteen I found out that I had been adopted. It was shortly after my father had died. My mother was cleaning out the safe and ran across the adoption papers. She said to me, 'I know that we should have told you earlier but we didn't. Your father was so afraid that you would go in search of your birth parents. We waited a very long time for you to come into our lives. I told him that you had that right, but he was so afraid that you might want to leave us.' I told her: "That's nuts. Why would I leave you after all you have done for me?" She went on, 'That's what I tried to tell him, but he insisted that we not tell you. I think that if we made any mistakes in raising you, that would definitely be one.'"

"Did you ever try to find your birth mother?" Tyler was curious.

"No, I thought about it but didn't act on it. Dori, my adoptive mother, told me that she met my birth mother. 'She wanted you to have the best that the world has to offer. She wanted you to be loved, well taken care of, and well-educated. It wasn't easy for her, Christopher. She loved you very much.' My birth mother named me Christopher. My adoptive parents liked that name. Mother thought it had strength and kindness. That's how I was raised, to be strong and kind. My father's name became my middle name and so I was christened Christopher Matthew Girrardi."

"You were greatly loved by your adoptive parents. You were so fortunate."

"Next time out, you tell me your story, okay?"

"There's not much to tell."

Sensing that now wasn't the time to get Tyler to talk about his childhood, Christopher took the bottle of cabernet and refilled Tyler's glass, then his. "Let's finish this bottle of wine."

Not much was said between the two men on the ride back home. Christopher drove up to Tyler's house. As Tyler reached with his right hand to open the door, Christopher used his right hand and grabbed Tyler's left. "Not so fast. Thank you for this evening. I thought it went well."

"Yes, it did, but remember it wasn't a date.

"How about dinner at my house next Friday? I'm not the cook that you are, but I do alright with grilling steaks."

"Ummm. Thanks, but I'm busy next Friday. I have my message circle."

With a puzzled look on his face, "What's that?"

"Some close friends and I get together and give each other messages from Spirit. It's what we intuit."

"I don't know anything about that. You'll have to enlighten me. You can do that over dinner at my place on Saturday at 6:00. Okay?"

He is persistent, I must say.

"I'll call you this week and give you the address. Say yes. Please."

"Okay, sure. Yes. Thank you."

Then Christopher reached across the console and with both arms pulled Tyler into him and hugged him tightly. He buried his neck into Tyler's, drinking in the scent.

Tyler couldn't help but note how good Christopher's scent smelled to him. *I hope he doesn't think I'm wearing too much cologne tonight.*

Releasing Tyler, Christopher winked, "Calvin Klein's Escape. It's awesome on you."

Shocked at Christopher's accurate scent detection, all Tyler could muster was, "It is! Thank you. See you next Saturday. Talk soon."

As Tyler walked up the walk to his front door, he thought, *I must be a magnet for men who need to figure out who they are.* Tyler smiled to himself as he unlocked his front door and greeted Sadie who eagerly awaited his return.

CHAPTER THIRTEEN

Magda was hosting the message circle at her home on Friday evening. It was Magda who introduced Tyler and Sophie and the other students in the area to metaphysics, to connecting with Spirit Guides and developing their intuition. The message circles were always enlightening. Magda opened with a prayer followed by a meditation. The prayer was the calling in of the Higher Power, whatever that was to the individual, and included invoking the Light, the Angels, Masters, Teachers, and Loved Ones. Each person present was the recipient of messages from the others in the group that evening. Everyone was encouraged to give messages to the others. "Give it even if it is just a word, a color, a symbol. Just because you don't know what it means, doesn't mean the recipient won't know what it means to him or her. Don't edit. Just give what you are sensing." Magda was a great medium and teacher, and her development classes were always full.

When it was Tyler's turn to receive messages, Magda asked him if there was an area or an issue that he wanted them to consider when listening to Spirit. His answer was, "Whatever Spirit wants and needs me to know." He received messages about peace, prosperity, business, and travel--specifically Italy in the future. When her students finished what they were intuiting, Magda started to talk. "There is a new romantic relationship for you. It is with someone you already know. If he hasn't made this known to you yet, he will very soon." Magda paused to listen to her guides. "No, Spirit says he has made it known to you."

Tyler couldn't really say he was surprised as Christopher had been upfront with him prior to their spending time together getting to know one another. For some reason, he kept telling himself that he wasn't enough and that Christopher would soon back off. It just hadn't happened yet. *But I think that Magda is talking about Christopher, not Ben, whom he still pined for, if the truth were known.*

The students in the circle listened intently as Magda gave Tyler his message. Much could be learned from observing her method of working.

Tyler hadn't said a word about Christopher to anyone. Yet Magda's insight didn't surprise him. "You need to take a close look at this potential relationship before you decide if you want to pursue it or not. This man is a good man; he has a kind heart. He is taller than you, very handsome, has a commanding presence when he enters a room." Magda paused again as if looking at an image. "Now my Guides are showing me a book that you are reading. This is a metaphor. You are almost finished with this book. There are only a few pages left. You put the book down because you don't want to finish reading it because then that story will be over. However, you already know in your heart how the story ends. It doesn't end the way you wanted it to, but you must finish this book before you can begin a new one." Magda paused as she continued to listen and look at what Spirit was telling and showing her. "I see the Phoenix waiting in the background. We have discussed this symbol before. You know what it means. You understand this?"

"Yes, Magda. I do. Thank you. Thank you, everyone, for your messages."

On the way home, Sophie was full of questions. "So who is the guy you have met? You haven't said anything. How come?"

"There's nothing to say. We've gone out a few times." He paused, "I have been seeing Christopher Girrardi."

"You have gone out with Christopher a few times and you haven't said anything? You always tell me everything."

"There's nothing to tell. He's nice. He's kind and he seems to like me as a friend."

"Of course. Why wouldn't he? Don't sell yourself short with him, Tyler."

"He's trying to find his way with the gay thing, but I am NOT sleeping with him."

"A new tact for you."

"Thank you, I think. After the Ben thing I'm gun-shy, I guess. Look how that turned out."

"I give that marriage of his a year to last, tops."

"Whatever. That doesn't matter. For some odd reason he doesn't want or still can't be with me. If it doesn't work out with Jacqueline, he'll find some other dumb bitch with money to woo. He's very good at bullshit you know. Pretending that he likes you and getting you to fall in love with him. Then because you love him and you think that he loves you, because ministers, of all people, don't lie about anything, especially love, you start to give lots of money to his church. Then you discover it's all based on bullshit."

"You fell in love with him because you wanted to."

Sighing deeply, "Yes, I did."

"For your own peace of mind Tyler, tell Ben *adios*. He's not good enough for you. Finish the 'book' that Magda talked about, and let Ben go."

Sophie pulled into Tyler's driveway and they hugged each other good night. Tyler got out of Sophie's car. "See you in the morning. Sweet dreams. And Sophie, thanks for being my friend."

CHAPTER FOURTEEN

The next evening, Saturday, Tyler made his way onto the winding driveway that led to Christopher's house. Christopher had sent him a note midweek with his address and directions. Although Christopher had said he would call, he didn't. *That's okay*, thought Tyler, even though he had secretly looked forward to getting another call from Christopher. It was nice to be the object of someone's attention even if it wasn't coming from the one he still secretly wanted it to be.

Tyler had delivered flowers to other houses in this area before. The whole area had huge homes, all five to six bedrooms, three-stall garages, some with pools, some with tennis courts, several with both. A few were over-looking beautiful Lake Michigan. Big homes for people with big incomes who lived at the country club, traveled all over, threw lavish parties. They lived in a much different world than Tyler. The whole subdivision consisted of winding roads, many ending in a cul-de-sac with a huge home positioned at the end. Such was Christopher's abode.

When Tyler pulled up in front of Christopher's sprawling two-story house, he thought, *Okay, Cinderella. You have to leave by midnight.* The contemporary house was a light gray trimmed in white with dark gray shingles. The entrance had two white columns supporting an extended roof over the front steps. Dormer windows accented the second story. From the outside it looked as if the style of windows let lots of light into the interior. A three-stall attached garage was at the right end. Low-growing evergreen shrubbery graced the entire width of the impressive recently built home. *I doubt that this is even five years old. He lives here alone? It's a big house for one person.*

Tyler grabbed the bottle of shiraz wine he had brought as a host gift and walked up the well-landscaped sidewalk and approached the double front oak doors. Just as he reached to push the doorbell, Christopher opened the door, beaming, "You came. You found it."

"Of course I came. I said I would. Your directions made it easy to find. Here, this is for you," Tyler said, handing Christopher the bottle of wine.

"Thanks, we'll have this with dinner. Would you like the grand tour?"

"Sure. Which wing do you live in?"

"Come on, it's not that big."

The beautiful home boasted hardwood floors with area rugs throughout. Christopher showed him the formal living room which featured two identical beige sofas with lots of throw pillows. The sofas, perpendicular to the stone fireplace with a white mantle, faced each other with a trunk-like table separating them. The snow white walls seemed to Tyler to give it a cold feeling. Next, Christopher ushered him into the great room. The warm cherry paneling and ceilings made it very attractive. A wide-screen television was mounted on the wall above the fireplace. A brocade sofa and table faced the fireplace. Two leather arm chairs graced the

French doors leading outside. There were built-in bookcases on either end of the fireplace. "This is my favorite room. I spend a lot of time here."

"I can see why. I would too, if I were you."

The formal dining room was painted dark blue. The white crown molding and ceiling accompanied the décor. A long table with six chairs covered in white brocade fabric were around the table. "I have extra leaves to extend the table. It will comfortably seat twelve."

"A nice number for a dinner party."

"That's what I thought, although I haven't entertained much since I lived here."

The door to the kitchen was at one end of the dining room. When Tyler walked in he gasped, "Oh, my!" He had only seen pictures of kitchens like this one in magazines. White cabinets contrasted with the dark gray granite counter tops. Gray ceramic tile created the backsplash behind the sink and the commercial size stove with two large ovens. Clear light fixtures were suspended from the ceiling via antique brass chains and provided the main lighting. Valences above the window were the only window treatments providing a very inviting area to prepare meals. "Look at all of this counter space! Christopher, this is a great house for entertaining. You must have large, lovely parties here."

"That's the intention, but it hasn't happened yet. Let me show you the upstairs." As they exited the other end of the kitchen, they went by the breakfast nook containing an oak table and four chairs. The view looked out on the back yard and pool. *A great spot for morning coffee,* thought Tyler.

"The upstairs was originally intended to be all bedrooms but I've changed that a bit." Opening one door so Tyler could look in he could see Christopher's home office, complete with a cherry desk and leather furniture. Another room had been converted to a small gym with free weights and several exercise machines.

Then Christopher ushered Tyler into his bedroom. The king-size bed and triple dresser dominated the room. "On this side is the dressing area which has a walk-in closet." There were still a few items of women's clothing hanging. Tyler tried not to stare at them but Christopher saw his look. "They belong to my ex. I guess she forgot about them. I need to get rid of them."

"Christopher, you don't owe me any explanations."

"I know."

"So show me the bathroom."

Christopher led the way into the master bathroom. A large brass faucet was by the white Jacuzzi tub. On the other side of the room was a walk-in shower large enough for three people. Plush white and gold towels hung near the shower and adjacent to the vanity.

"Two sinks. Designed for 'his and hers'."

"Or 'his and his'," countered Christopher.

No curtains were hanging and the view of the trees at the property's edge from this upper level was beautiful.

"Your house is magnificent, Christopher."

"Thanks. It's getting there. I could use some help with the finishing touches to make it better."

Okay. *Where are the curtains and bedspread?* Tyler wondered.

As if reading his mind, Christopher answered, "I took down the curtains that my soon-to-be ex-wife had up. I want something a little more masculine-looking. Maybe you can help me with that and find a comforter to match. You certainly have an eye for what looks good."

"This is a lot of house for just one person."

"Yeah." Christopher's voice trailed off.

Outside there was a beautiful patio with a built-in barbecue, nothing like the Webber gas grill on wheels that Tyler could afford. Adjacent to the patio was a large swimming pool with pool side chairs, life preservers, and huge plants in terra cotta pots. It was a beautiful estate, Tyler had to admit.

Christopher led Tyler to the other end of the patio. "Tyler, look at this."

"Wow! That is one serious looking telescope. Are you into astronomy?"

"It's a hobby. I find great solace in looking at the stars and the constellations. I just got it. It's a new toy."

"May I?"

"Sure."

Tyler looked into the telescope, somewhat taken aback at how close the constellations and millions of stars now appeared. It was the perfect, clear night to observe.

"Tyler, have you ever felt like you really don't belong? Don't fit in anywhere?"

"Yes, all the time, and that isn't just about being gay. It's also about being on my spiritual journey. Most people think I'm into the occult, which really means the unknown. Those people have closed minds. One has to be open to learn about anything."

"Besides that, have you ever felt that you didn't really belong here?"

"You mean here on earth? I believe that human beings are really spiritual beings having a physical experience on this planet in this school called 'life.' Is that what you mean?"

"Yes, I guess so. I just know that when I look at the stars, I feel a sense of homesickness, like that is where I came from, like the stars are my true home. Do you think that's weird or a little crazy?"

Laughing, "You're asking me, a person who talks to dead people, if that's crazy?" Tyler was mesmerized. Suddenly he didn't see Christopher as this 6'2", 230 pound, handsome football jock. He was so much more than that! He was talking to Tyler about something he found fascinating and could totally relate to.

"Have you ever heard of the Star People?"

"People whose ancestry is the stars? Yes, I've read a little about it." Christopher replied. "I've never said that out loud before."

"My good friend and spiritual teacher, Magda, talked about the Star People recently in one of the classes she teaches. She's been doing research on the subject."

Magda's lectures were always intriguing. She had spoken on what was currently known. Those who came from the Star Nations will often feel like a stranger here on the planet earth. She said that many have very compelling eyes and a striking physical appearance. Christopher certainly was that. She also said those who originate from the Star People have a deep knowing that their true home is somewhere among the stars.

Nodding affirmatively, Christopher could only say, "Yes, yes."

"Do you believe in reincarnation?"

"I'm open to it."

"Do you believe in contact or communication with deceased loved ones?"

"I think so. I mean I KNOW sometimes my dad is talking to me. I can sense his presence even though he has been gone almost twenty-two years."

"That is music to my ears. Do you believe in miracles?"

"Yes. I think that it is a miracle that you are a part of my life."

"That is perhaps the nicest thing anyone has ever told me." Taking Christopher's hand in his, Tyler asked him if he by chance had ever had a life threatening illness.

"Why do you ask that?"

"That's often another characteristic of a Star Person."

"When I was ten, I contracted spinal meningitis. I remember being so sick, lying in a hospital bed, with a high fever."

Christopher paused.

"Can you tell me more, or is it too painful?"

Christopher recounted the incident as if it happened yesterday. He saw someone in a white lab coat, a doctor he presumed, talking in hushed tones to his parents who were on either side of his bed, and they were crying.

"The anguished looks on their faces was too much to bear." Christopher recounted that he rose above it all and hovered above his body, but his parents were looking at him lying there in the bed. "I was kind of hovering above them like the Flying Nun. I felt so free and happy, and I wasn't sick anymore. There was a white shaft of light which I felt was an angelic presence who said I should follow him and go into the Light."

Tyler was riveted by this story.

Christopher asked the angel about his parents. "Can't they come with me?"

The voice within the Light said, "No. It isn't their time. You have been given a window of opportunity to make your transition. You can go into the Light now."

"I don't want to leave my Mother and Father. I love them, and they are so good to me. I don't want them to worry about me."

"That is a choice you can make now. Whichever you choose, it will be the right choice for this time."

"I want to go back home to my parents."

"Then it is done."

Christopher remembered slipping back into his body. His body ached slightly, but the fever was gone. He opened his eyes. When he did so, his mother yelled for the nurse to come immediately.

"He's opened his eyes. He's back with us!"

The nurse ran into the room and checked me over. "It's a miracle! He's pulled through this."

"My parents were crying and squeezing my hands, and I went back to sleep. When I woke up again, I felt so much better." Christopher took a deep breath.

"You had a near-death experience at age ten! Did you tell your parents about it?"

"I tried to a little later, but they felt that I had a very high fever and along with the meds, was imagining it all. To them, it really didn't matter because their prayers had been answered. I lived."

"Did you ever see or hear from that angel since then?"

"No. I hadn't really thought much about that whole ordeal until now, talking to you."

"I can't wait to introduce you to Magda. She'll love this story! She will have so much to ask you."

"Are you hungry?" Christopher asked. "I'm starved. How do you like your steak cooked?"

"Medium rare, please."

"Me, too. I'm beginning to think that we might have a lot more in common than either of us imagined."

"The Star Nations and the Star People are only one aspect of Spirituality and Metaphysics."

"I know. We have lots to know and to learn about each other, Tyler."

CHAPTER FIFTEEN

It was early Sunday afternoon and a beautiful fall day. Tyler was out taking Sadie for a walk when he got a text from Christopher. "What are you doing? Want to watch some football with me?"

Tyler texted back: "Sadie and I are out for a walk. I know nothing about football so probably not the best bud for you to watch the game with."

An immediate response came: "I can explain it to you if you want to know. Bring Sadie with you."

"Sadie, we've been invited to a football game. Secretly I think Christopher thinks if he can get you to like him, he has an "in" with me. Want to watch football?"

Sadie was distracted by a squirrel running freely and was straining on the leash. "Leave the squirrel alone. He doesn't want to play with you. Come on. We're going to watch football with Chris." *Chris, hmmm, I've never called him that before. Well, that's because Chris is a good name for a football jock enthusiast, rather than Christopher. So maybe he's Chris today.*

They pulled up at Christopher's house, and he met them at the door smiling from ear to ear. "I didn't think that you'd really come."

"Why not? I said we would. Besides, you've been a good sport and do things that I enjoy. I can do this for you. Sadie, please don't make a mess anywhere."

Christopher led the way into the great room that held the wide-screen TV. The game was just about to start. On the table were a couple of bowls of chips and dip and a plate with crackers and cheese to snack on.

"Would you like a beer?"

"Beer? I mean, sure, beer," Tyler answered in a deep voice, mustering up all the machismo he could.

"I have wine if you'd rather. I just like to enjoy a beer when I watch football."

"I'll drink a beer. Thanks."

"What kind? I have a well-stocked bar."

"I don't suppose you have any Stella Artois?"

"Actually, I do. Be right back."

In no time Christopher was back with a Bud Light for himself and a Stella for Tyler.

"Thanks, Chris. Stella Artois. Sounds like the name of a drag queen doesn't it?

"I wouldn't know about that. Cheers," he said as they clinked their bottles together and sat down to watch the game. Sadie lay on the floor by Tyler's feet, engrossed with the rawhide chew he had brought for her.

The game was between the Colts and the Ravens, and the Indianapolis Colts were hosting. Tyler watched the screen, intently trying to figure out the game. He didn't want to sound as ignorant as he was about the game by asking a lot of stupid questions. He did know that a touchdown earned six points but sometimes when the ball was kicked over the goal post, it earned them one additional point and sometimes three. Finally, he asked Chris about it. Christopher explained it to him. The Colts were ahead 13-7, and Christopher was ecstatic by this score as were their fans in the stadium that afternoon. Finally, Christopher said, "That's twice that you have called me Chris instead of Christopher today. You always call me Christopher, never Chris. What's with that?"

"I just thought, well I probably think too much. I mean, I'm sure that when you played football, your teammates called you Chris, not Christopher, and we're watching football, which is something you seem to enjoy very much and, I don't know, it just seemed appropriate."

"I don't mind, but I do like it when you call me Christopher, because no one else does, Ty."

"If you're Chris, then I'm Ty?"

"That's right."

"Okay, but Sadie is still Sadie." At the mention of her name, Sadie looked up at the two men, decided everything was all right and returned her focus to her rawhide chew. They both laughed, and Christopher went to get them each another beer.

When Christopher returned with the beer, he asked, "Would you want to go with me some weekend to see a Colts game? That's my old stomping grounds. We could make a weekend of it. Maybe Sophie would watch Sadie for you. Just an idea."

"Ummm, sure. I've never been to a pro football game before. I actually like watching the game with you even though I don't understand all of the plays and what the refs are finding fault with some of the times."

Tyler paused a moment before stating, "When we go to the game, Christopher, I expect to pay for half of everything. You can't keep paying for everything all of the time. It's very kind of you, but I'm not comfortable with it."

"Okay, whatever you say. We'll have fun."

Just then Tyler got a text from Sophie. "Call me. It's Magda."

Tyler immediately called Sophie, who was crying. "I'm at the hospital with Magda. She's dying. She didn't tell anyone how sick she was. *'I'm fine--the body is not.'* Apparently the cancer has returned with a vengeance. The doctors can't understand why she isn't in great pain. She has refused all meds. She wants to see you. Please come."

Tyler was visibly shaken. "I'll be right there." Turning to Christopher, "I have to leave. That was Sophie. Our friend, Magda, is dying. I need to go now." Tyler started to tear up. *No tears, Tyler. Not now. Be strong. Get your shit together.*

Christopher couldn't help but notice Tyler's body language. "Let me drive you. Sadie can stay in the kitchen. We'll leave food and water for her. She can't hurt the floor if she has to go."

Christopher made a beeline for the kitchen and took out a new bag of dog food and poured some in a bowl. He also set a bowl of water out while Tyler took Sadie outside to do her thing. "That's a good girl, Sadie. Thanks for peeing and pooping when I need you to."

Back in the house, Tyler noticed that Christopher had the same brand of dog food that Tyler gave Sadie. "How did you know what brand of dog food to just happen to have on hand?"

"I paid attention to what you gave her when I was at your house. I bought a bag just in case. It's the Boy Scout in me. 'Be prepared.'"

On the way to the hospital, Tyler talked about Magda. Magda was short for Magdalene. She was a gifted psychic medium and had been a long time friend, teacher, and mentor of Tyler's. She would never discuss her illness and told herself that she had no pain. She never took the pain meds because Magda wanted to always have her wits about her. "Besides, I can't give messages and readings if my mind is clouded with pain killers. That is the work I'm here to do, and I will do it until it is time for me to transition." That's how she lived.

"I don't think that she even had an aspirin in her house."

When they got to the hospital, Sophie was waiting for them outside the door to Magda's room. Tyler formally introduced her to Christopher. "I was at Christopher's house when you sent me the message. He drove me. Besides, I want him to meet Magda."

"They're changing the bed and making her more comfortable. They're going to start an IV. She finally agreed to that much. I saw her yesterday. She called me late this morning. What a change in less than twenty-four hours."

The nurse came out. "You can go in now."

Sophie said, "You two go in. I told her you were on your way."

Tyler, not sure of what he was going to see, went in with Christopher closely behind him.

"Hello, sweetie." Taking her hand into his, Tyler asked, "Magda, why didn't you say something sooner?"

"There wasn't anything to say. If I had dwelled on the disease of the body, I wouldn't have lasted this long, and I had work to do."

"This is Christopher. He had a near-death experience when he was ten. I had intended for him to meet you and to tell you about it, but this is all happening so fast."

Magda raised her free hand, and Christopher embraced it with his two big hands. "Magda, Tyler has told me so much about you. You are indeed a very special lady. It's my pleasure to meet you."

Magda turned to Tyler as she released her hand from Christopher's grasp. "He has a good, firm handshake, Tyler. He has strong, vibrant energy. He's a good man. He's a keeper."

"I know."

Then in a loud whisper, "Don't fuck this up."

"Magda!"

"Keeping it real." To Christopher, "Take good care of my friend, Tyler. Don't take any shit from him."

Laughing, Christopher responded, "I promise you I won't."

"God, Magda, whose side are you on?"

"Yours, honey, always yours. But I know how you can be, how we can all be."

She closed her eyes. Christopher said, "I'm going to leave you two alone. I'll be outside in the hall if you need me."

"Have Sophie come in, please." The color was rapidly draining from Magda's face. Tyler squeezed her right hand. "I'm right here, Magda."

Sophie came in and took her place on the other side of the bed and held Magda's left hand.

Magda tried to open her eyes and then closed them. "I don't have much time left." Opening her eyes once more, "Thank you so much for being the children I never had. Promise me that you will continue to study and to meditate. Find another teacher. You are both good psychic mediums. You just have to trust." Again she closed her eyes.

"We love you," Tyler and Sophie said in unison.

After a few minutes of silence, Sophie said, "When you are ready, just go into the Light, Magda. Leave this body that no longer serves you as you begin the next leg of your journey."

Tyler then added, "The angels are here to help you cross over. God Bless you, Magda. Thank you for everything."

Magda's eyes remained closed. She had a bit of a smile as she murmured, "No more talking." A sigh, "I'm on my way out."

During the next few minutes, her breathing became shallower and less frequent.

Then Magda opened her eyes, smiled, and said, "I'm ready. I'm going Home now."

And she went. As her last breath exhaled from her tired, thin body, both Sophie and Tyler saw the bright flash of white light leave Magda's brow and shoot through the ceiling and disappear into the ethers.

Magda went Home.

CHAPTER SIXTEEN

It was a couple weeks after Magda's memorial service, and Tyler and Christopher were headed to Indianapolis for the Colts game. They had left early on a Saturday morning and would drive directly there. The game wasn't until Sunday afternoon, but Christopher wanted to leave on Saturday. "We're going to have the best time, Tyler. Just wait." Tyler was quiet as Christopher cruised along, varying the speed between seventy-five and eighty the entire time they were on the divided highway. For this trip, they were riding in Christopher's burgundy Mercedes. One of his self-indulgences was to have a variety of cars to choose from for their outings.

I love being chauffeured, thought Tyler. His thoughts then changed to the probable sleeping arrangements that he undoubtedly would have to deal with at the motel or hotel or where ever Christopher made reservations. At Christopher's insistence, he was taking care of everything that weekend, meals and lodging, tickets. "The next weekend getaway is on you, okay? This was my idea, so it's on me."

Tyler's mind was on overdrive. *What the hell is wrong with you, Tyler? Ben is not ever going to come to his senses and come back to you. It's been almost a year since you have even seen him, so why can't you just let him go and move on? Soulmate or not, he doesn't want you. Even if he did, did he ever treat you with the respect, the kindness, the generosity, the infinite patience and kindness that Christopher has these last six months? Of course not. What are you afraid of? Afraid he'll fuck you and dump you? Or are you afraid that he will stay? Afraid that he will find out about your sordid past? How could he? How could he not if he wanted to?*

"What are you so deep in thought about, Ty?"

"Just daydreaming." A moment lapsed when Tyler asked, "Did you just call me Ty?"

"It's football weekend. You know, I'm Chris and you're Ty? Remember?"

"Okay, Chris," Tyler was smiling as he replied.

As they were driving along the highway, Tyler noticed the sign stating that Indianapolis, home of the Colts, was only eighty miles away. "You know that there is a little town called Chesterfield not far from here. They have a Spiritualist community there known as Camp Chesterfield. We have time. Do you think we could stop there and visit? Maybe walk around and see what they have to offer?" Tyler knew that there might be a gala that Saturday evening where several of the psychic mediums demonstrated their mediumship, utilizing various modalities. He and/or Christopher might be lucky enough to receive a message or two from loved ones.

"Sure. We have time. No set plans for this evening. We can be spontaneous. I like that, sometimes," was Christopher's reply.

"Thanks for indulging me. It might be fun to go to the gala tonight. We might each get a message, or not. It all depends on if Spirit wants us to have one."

"Sounds interesting. I want to learn more about the message work you refer to." Christopher was also beginning to wonder if

Tyler was ever going to come around. Yes, he enjoyed his company very much, and Tyler was a good sport about going with him and indulging him with his passion for football. Nevertheless, he thought he'd been very patient with him. Was he still hung up over that minister, Ben? Christopher didn't want to tell him that Ben had come on to him shortly after the one time that he and Karen had visited that church, which also must have been during the time that Tyler and Ben were an item. He thought then that Ben was a douche bag. There was just something about him that he didn't like.

Christopher pointed toward a road sign. "Rest area up ahead. I need to pee and stretch my legs."

Tyler agreed, "Yeah, me too."

When they got back in to the car, Christopher made no attempt to start the engine. He looked straight ahead.

"What's up?" Tyler queried.

"Tyler, I have to ask you something. Whatever the answer is, it's not going to change this weekend or what I've planned for us." Pausing to take a deep breath Christopher asked, "Are you not attracted to me at all? I know when we started seeing each other, it was to get to know each other, become friends, which we have done. Call it what you want to, we have been dating each other. Albeit, dating without sex."

Tyler started to say something but Christopher gestured for him to be quiet. He was on a roll. "Yes, I know you said we were never going to have sex with each other. You were very upfront, and I respected that. Nonetheless, I have to be honest with you. I want more. I want to make love to you."

Reality suddenly set in to Tyler's brain. *All your life you have waited for someone to say those words to you Tyler. Why did you still think it might be Ben and not Christopher?* He turned to face his ardent suitor.

Christopher continued. "I want more than this. I love spending time with you. I think you like me. You don't care for sports, but you watch the games with me. You're going with me this weekend to a football game for Christ's sake. I feel that I have been a good friend to you as well. I have been there for you when you needed me. For example, when Magda died and her funeral, I was at your side. Now you want to take a side trip to Camp Chesterfield, which is fine. I do want to know more about spirituality and metaphysics. But I…"

Tyler cut Christopher off. "Yes, you have. You have been the best friend to me, and I do appreciate it. I also acknowledge I have been lax in acknowledging that fact. I'm sorry."

"I don't know how much longer I can do this if you don't want to really be with me in every sense of the word. Is there something that I've said or done or do that you can't stand the thought of getting intimate with me? If there is anything, please tell me. I can take it."

"You haven't done a thing to warrant that."

"I want you so much!"

Tyler forced himself to look directly into Christopher's eyes. *This brave man is putting himself on the line for you, Tyler!*

"I'm a big boy. If you don't want to explore going to the next level with me, then I don't know, I guess I have to move on."

There was a long awkward silence. Tyler couldn't think of a thing to say that would make this situation go away.

"Just please tell me something."

Well, Tyler thought, better to have this conversation here than in the motel faced with one queen-sized bed.

"Christopher, you have been unwavering with kindness and patience. You're an incredibly sensitive, strong, and brave man. You're a man's man. You're the total package. I haven't been fair to you. I have been caught up in my own shit all of the time." Tyler took a deep breath and continued. "Most of the time I have been carrying a torch for Ben." Tyler was surprised at his vocal admission to himself as well as to Christopher. *There I said it out loud.* "You're much more of a man, more of a decent human being than he ever was. I have never had anyone in my life treat me the way you have. You listen to me. You totally get me. You're kind and generous to a fault."

"Then what's the problem?"

"Maybe I'm afraid that you will be so disappointed with the whole sex thing with me. I also know that once a man comes out as gay sexually, then 99% of the time he soon turns into a little kid in a candy shop, wanting to try out all of the kinds of candy, getting a taste of everything. That scares me a little about you. I know that I also don't want to be your guinea pig. Maybe I'm afraid that you won't like me if you know *everything* about me. What if I really like making love to you, but that I don't satisfy you, then what? I'm scared of that."

"Please don't be scared of that or of me. Please."

"I knew that one day we'd have to have this conversation. Thank you for being the adult here and bringing it up." Tyler looked away and stared out the window to his right.

"Okay," was all Christopher could say in response as he started the engine.

As they drove through the entrance marked Camp Chesterfield, Tyler could immediately feel the incredible and powerful shift in the energy. Christopher parked by the bookstore, and they went in and browsed around.

"Are you new to the Camp?" the smiling cashier asked.

"Yes," chimed both Tyler and Christopher in unison.

"Help yourself to the brochures. The museum is open today. There is a gala tonight with four of our excellent mediums giving messages. All of it is by donation only."

"What time is the gala?" Tyler asked.

"7:00 p.m. sharp."

Tyler looked at Christopher, who nodded yes, of course. "I want to see what it's all about."

Pamphlets in hand, the two men left the bookstore and ventured into the nearby business district. Soon they found a small restaurant in town and grabbed a quick bite to eat.

As they headed back towards Camp Chesterfield, the traffic was noticeably heavier. It looked like there would be a full house tonight at the gala. When they entered the chapel at 6:30, Tyler led the way towards the front. "I do not want to sit in the front row, Tyler."

"We won't, but we should sit in the front third of the pews. I think that will give us a better chance at getting a message from one of the mediums."

They sat about four rows back from the front. The first medium was introduced as Reverend Elizabeth, a dark-haired, middle-aged woman who would be demonstrating flower messages. Next to her on the platform was a large vase containing a mixed bouquet of roses, gerber daisies, snapdragons, and lilies along with some ferns and other greenery. Reverend Elizabeth gave a couple of messages to others. For her third message, she pulled out a red rose. Reverend Elizabeth stepped off of the platform and came down the aisle and stopped near Tyler. "Hello, young man. This message is for you. There is a new romance in your life isn't there? It's there if you let it in. Spirit is telling me that you are holding back for some reason. Only you KNOW that reason. This is an issue you really need to address because Spirit is saying you are letting this 'stuff' interfere with what you truly want, which is to be in a committed relationship. Would you understand this?"

Tyler mouthed the word "yes."

She continued, "The thorns on this stem represent the pain you have suffered from others in past relationships. Do you notice how when we look at the rose, we just see its beauty? If we start at the base of the stem and work our way past the thorns, we arrive at the petals that make up the flower which is what we see at first glance. We only see the thorns when we closely examine the entire flower. Observe that this rose is really in the bud stage and is starting to open. It can't stay in the bud forever, because it would be too painful; it has to open and blossom. This loving relationship which is at your door is in the budding stage. You have to allow it to open, or you will remain in pain as the bud would if it didn't allow nature to take its course and open to all its magnificence and beauty. Blessings to you, my dear one."

"Thank you," Tyler said softly. He was afraid to look at Christopher. His message concerned him as well.

The next medium sat in a cabinet and gave channeled messages via his Spirit Guide, a Native American energy. The cabinet consisted of a box-like square framework made of pipes. Four pipes formed the corner poles. There were curtain panels of dark red fabric that served as the walls. The cabinet was just large enough to contain a chair in which the medium sat. Once seated, the front curtain panel was closed so that the medium's energy, when joined by Spirit, would be contained in that small space. It would make it easier for the medium to channel the information that Spirit was giving him. He channeled messages to the entire congregation about respecting Mother Earth and the need for taking better care of her. "You are each a steward of this beautiful planet that you incarnated on." Christopher found it all fascinating.

The last message bearer of the evening gave flame messages. He held a piece of paper, which looked like a blank three-inch by five-inch index card, just above the candle's flame so that the heat would produce enough smoke, and various images would occur on the card. From those images, the readings came forth. This medium, Reverend Don, a white-haired man who was every bit of seventy, came to Christopher for his first message of the evening. "May I have your name please?"

"Christopher."

"Christopher, I would like to touch in with you if I might. The image I see here is like that of a snake shedding its skin. We know that when a serpent sheds its skin, it symbolizes growth and transformation. The old skin didn't fit anymore. You have been growing by leaps and bounds in your personal life, big changes. 'Lifestyle' is the word I'm hearing."

Smiling warmly, the reader looked to Christopher for confirmation, and Christopher nodded "yes."

"I'm also looking at this next image which looks to me like a lightning bolt. Do you see that as I do?" he asked, holding the card near Christopher's line of vision.

"Yes, I do."

"There has been a disruption in your life as you knew it. A change is in the process, a change for the better. You will be happier if you go with it' and I feel that you have started on this new path, which is so very new for you. You are in uncharted waters, so to speak. Does this make sense to you?""Oh, yes, it does. It's very clear to me."

"I see stumbling blocks in front of you. Either climb over them, or go around, but do not go back. You can do this." Reverend Don paused to listen again to what he was being told. "It's a wide road ahead of you I see. This applies to your work and to your personal life as well. Your spiritual life is just taking off as well. How exciting for you! God bless."

"God bless you, too. Thank you," said Christopher. To Tyler, Christopher whispered, "Wow, these people are amazing!"

"I'm glad you liked it." Tyler knew all too well what the meaning of these messages applied to both of them. Soon, he would have to have a heart-to-heart with Christopher and tell him that he was just too scared to have a full-fleged relationship with him. He had been avoiding it, thinking that it wouldn't be necessary. *Why did everything have to get so complicated?*

As they left Camp Chesterfield and headed towards the motel, Christopher asked, "Are you hungry? I'm famished."

"That does sound good. I could go for a little something and a glass of chardonnay."

They drove along for a distance before spotting a sign that read, "Libations, Sustenance and Enlightenment Within." "Let's stop there," said Tyler, "it looks kind of interesting."

Christopher made a right turn into the parking lot. Soon they were inside with wine in front of them and sandwiches ordered. The establishment, known as Mona's, featured a piano bar. Mona played the piano and sang. She was pleasant to listen to. However, she entertained requests from other customers who got up and took over the microphone and sang while Mona accompanied them. The two customers who were up there were bad. First, one woman sang "Desperado." Then a middle-aged guy tried to sing "Blue Bayou."

Reading the expression on Tyler's face, Christopher told him, "Give them credit for trying. They are uninhibited, but more importantly, they are enjoying themselves."

"You're right, but they are so bad."

"Don't be so critical unless you can get up there and can do better."

"I don't think so."

"Why not? Sing a song for me."

Tyler thought a moment. "All right, I will."

Tyler abruptly got up and went over to Mona when she had finished the song she was playing and asked her, "Could I please sing with you?"

"Sure, honey. If I know it, I'll play it for you."

"Do you know 'Me and Bobby McGee?' by Kristofferson and Foster?"

"Love that one. Do Miss Joplin proud, honey."

Tyler took the microphone. As Mona played the introduction, he closed his eyes and thought, "Creator, let me be as good as I can possibly be."

Tyler knew immediately as the first few lyrics came out of his mouth where he was going with this song. He was thinking of Ben, of how happy he'd always thought that he and Ben could have been together, and how, now, he really hoped that Ben had found some happiness. Surprisingly, these thoughts came easily and were very freeing. His threw his entire body into communicating what he felt the song writers had intended to be understood by this timeless piece.

Christopher was taken aback at how throaty Tyler made his voice. With all due respect to Janis Joplin, Tyler was making this song his. He put his entire being into it. Tyler was singing publically for the first time in almost a year, and he was in another dimension. It felt good, so good to him. Christopher couldn't help but notice that the other patrons in the restaurant stopped talking and eating to listen to this young man at the microphone.

At the song's conclusion, the applause from the patrons brought Tyler back to reality. He took a subtle bow before triumphantly walking back to the table. Once there, he was warmly embraced by one beaming Christopher Girrardi.

CHAPTER SEVENTEEN

They checked into the hotel room, which contained one king-size bed. All Christopher said as he emerged from the bathroom wearing his boxer briefs was, "Which side of the bed do you want?"

"The left, I guess," replied Tyler, as he stripped off his tee shirt. *When he sees my flabby body, that will turn him off,* thought Tyler. "Christopher, if I start to snore, you can hit me to make me stop."

"I'm not going to hit you ever. I might jostle you, however," he said with a grin.

Tyler lay on his left side facing the wall, the sheet pulled up over him, wishing he could fall asleep and that morning would be here. He felt Christopher shift his weight in the bed and could soon tell by his breathing that he was asleep.

Tyler had a talk with himself. *You have to make a decision soon. Christopher has shown you infinite patience, treats you like royalty, and is someone anybody, male or female, would feel lucky to be with. You used to jump into bed with anyone for money and/or for fun. Why then can't you have sex with Christopher? Because he is a good man and you don't want to hurt him, and you really don't deserve him.* The discussion within his brain continued. *Just have sex with him, and he'll get you out of his system. He'll never have to know about your past. Yes, that's it. I'll pretend to want to have sex with him, he'll see that it isn't all that great with me, and he'll drop me and I won't feel hurt because I knew all along what I was doing. Yup, that is the plan of action.*

Tyler felt pleased that he had figured out what he would do. As soon as he had, his whole body seemed to relax. He closed his eyes ready to slumber. Just as he did, Christopher rolled over in his sleep and threw his right arm over and around Tyler and pressed his muscular, hairy chest against Tyler's back. Tyler smiled to himself, lightly kissed the top of Christopher's hand and relaxed into sleep as he felt Christopher's warm breath on his neck and head. However, what Tyler did not see was the big smile on Christopher's face as he snuggled up to Tyler and fell back asleep.

The rest of the weekend went smoothly and uneventfully. They had a good time dining out; the Colts game was fun. Christopher enjoyed explaining the plays to Tyler. Tyler really was happy to see how happy Christopher was at this game. To his own surprise, he was really enjoying the game as well. Tyler liking football? Who knew?! Just as Christopher had told him earlier, he wasn't going to let Tyler's lack of interest in him change the weekend. Obviously, he was a man of his word.

The following Saturday was a black-tie event at the country club. An acquaintance of Christopher's was hosting a fund-raiser for a charity. Tyler hadn't paid much attention to what it was for. Christopher had said he really needed to put in an appearance, and he didn't really see why Tyler wouldn't go with him. He was quite emphatic that he didn't want to go alone either.

"Christopher, thank you for the offer, but black-tie events are always so stuffy."

"They don't have to be. Have you ever been to one, other than to deliver flowers?"

"No."

"Well, then you don't really know. You're being judgmental."

"There is a big difference between being judgmental and being discerning."

"Oh, really? I didn't know that. I did rent a tux for you, so you can't say you don't have anything to wear. We can have fun if we want to. Both of us dressed to the nines."

"I don't think so."

"You know, you really are becoming kind of stuffy yourself, Tyler. Maybe you should try being a little more spontaneous once in awhile," Christopher chided him teasingly.

"What if the tux doesn't fit? You don't know my size."

"Oh, but I do. While you were in the shower last weekend at the hotel, I checked out your shoe, shirt, and pant size that you wore. There should be no problem with it fitting."

"You went to all of that trouble? Okay, I'll go."

"I'll pick you up at 6 p.m. sharp."

Tyler did look good in the tux. He had been getting up an hour earlier every morning and working out. He would never have the body that Christopher did, but then that wasn't his goal. He admittedly felt better and had more energy as a result.

Christopher was there at 6 o'clock sharp and looked like a million bucks. *Hell, he'd look good in burlap,* Tyler thought.

"We'll be the two most handsome men there, Tyler," Christopher said.

When they got there, Christopher promptly got them drinks. "Have a glass of wine. Relax," Christopher said.

They made their way through the gathering crowd, some of whom Tyler knew as customers from the store. Others he knew from his Church of the Open Door experience. He introduced Christopher to those he knew, and Christopher did likewise to his acquaintances.

Tyler relaxed when he saw Carmella. She came up to him and gave him a big hug. "Darling, Tyler, so good to see you here! Christopher, good to see you, too. You both look so handsome! Have fun, boys. Talk more later."

Christopher said so only Tyler could hear, "Have fun, boys. What was that about?"

"She wants us to have fun. That's all. Besides, we're going to be spontaneous tonight, aren't we?" Tyler said laughing and poking Christopher jokingly.

They mingled around, chatting, making small talk. There were approximately fifty items on tables as part of a silent auction. Items ranged from a $100 gift card good at Tyler's Floral & Gifts to a weekend stay with theater tickets for two at a plush hotel, dinner gift certificates, and other varied items. Christopher had purchased and donated the gift card from Tyler's.

Tyler said he didn't want to bid on anything. Christopher did bid on a few items that caught his eye. There was a live band which was taking requests. Up until then, they had been playing a hodgepodge of everything. Few people were dancing. Christopher had left Tyler under the premise of getting them each another glass of wine.

In the interim, Ben and his wife walked by. Welcoming the opportunity, Tyler spoke to them. "Ben, how are you? Jacqueline. I haven't seen you since you were in the shop to order flowers for your wedding. What's it been, a little over a year, already?"

"Yes, just over a year," Ben said guardedly.

"You should come to church some Sunday," Jacqueline piped in, not knowing what to say, sensing some awkwardness between her husband and Tyler.

"Been there, done that. It just doesn't really work for me."

"That's unfortunate because there was a time when it seemed to do so, but to each his own," Ben replied flashing his standard smile.

Then changing the subject, "Tyler, are you here alone?"

"No, I'm with Christopher Girrardi. He brought me. He went to get me a glass of wine."

Ben looked shocked. "You *came with* Christopher?"

"That's right, Ben. I'm WITH him."

Just then Christopher returned with a glass of wine in hand for Tyler and a Manhattan for himself. "Christopher, do you know Ben and Jacqueline? Ben is the minister at the Church of the Open Door."

"Yes, we've met once before. Nice to see both of you again." Christopher radiated his natural charm. "If you will excuse us, I need to speak to Tyler a moment."

"I just requested that the band play a polka. Do you know how to polka? I haven't danced that in a looooong time."

"You want me to dance a polka here with you at the country club? The Old Guard will throw us out. Is that what you want?"

"They won't throw us out, but it will liven up this party. You haven't answered my question, because if you can't polka, I'm going to look ridiculous out there by myself."

Tyler looked amused and shocked at the same time. This man never ceased to amaze him.

"Let's be spontaneous, Tyler."

"Even if it's a little crazy?"

"Especially if it's a little crazy, or even a lot crazy."

"Actually, I do know how to polka.

The band started to play the "Beer Barrel Polka.""You lead, Tyler."

Grinning at his handsome date, "Okay."

Tyler put his left hand around Christopher's waist and his right hand into Christopher's left, looked him directly into his irresistible blue eyes, and said, "One, two, three, let's go, handsome."

"Yes, sir."

And they were off. Tyler was keenly aware of the shocked looks from the others in the room as he and Christopher took over the dance floor. Eventually, a few other couples joined them on the floor. Tyler lost track of them. The room became a blur as they danced and spun around the dance floor. The two men were having the time of their lives, showing each other that he was anything but stuffy.

They were oblivious to any derogatory remarks made by the conservatives under their breaths. Jacqueline Thompson wasn't afraid to be heard. "I guess now we know the real reason why the Girarrdis got divorced. Why on earth would that handsome Christopher Girrardi be carrying on with that faggot florist? Obviously, he's never been with a real woman."

Ben Thompson cut his wife off. "Where did your homophobia come from? Tyler was a very valued member of our congregation. He was valued not only for what he gave fiscally but by what he contributed to us in his presence, his demeanor, his talents. Many of us cared for him deeply. We were saddened by the fact that he stopped attending."

"Do tell, Ben."

"Don't ever refer to him again in that degrading manner."

"Sure, Ben, whatever." Jacqueline Thompson could not have cared less about Tyler or what her husband really thought. She had no idea that her husband was a little jealous of the fun that Christopher and Tyler were having.

At one point in the dance, Tyler and Christopher released each other's hands, opened up and with arms around each other's waist, and danced forward to the rhythm for a few measures. Then instinctively, each pivoted back so he was facing his partner, re-joined hands, and continued to spin around the room. When the music stopped, they had to hang on to each other briefly in order to get their footing back. Christopher looked into Tyler's eyes and smiled. "That was fun! I had no idea that you knew how to polka that well."

"Once in awhile I like to surprise you."

Carmella came running up to them. "Tyler, you certainly outdid the Charleston at my party last year! Christopher, you certainly know how to cut the rug! What fun to watch you two out there."

"Thanks, Carmella," the dancers said in unison.

"One just needs a good partner," Tyler added. As they made their way through the crowed he said, "Let's go outside and get some fresh air."

"Sure." They found their way to the patio. The cool air felt good as they had both worked up a sweat.

Saying nothing, they both looked up at the clear night sky. Stars were out in great abundance. "Your people are smiling down at us, Christopher."

"It appears that way. I think they approve."

Tyler, taking Christopher's hand in his said, "Christopher, would you please take me home now?"

"Something wrong? It's not that late."

"Nothing's wrong. I want to dance with you alone at my house. Only this time it will be a slow dance."

Saying nothing other than nodding his head "yes," Christopher and Tyler walked hand in hand to the car. Christopher unlocked the passenger side and let Tyler in first, like any gentleman would on a date.

When they got home, Sadie greeted them warmly. Tyler let her out for a few minutes while he turned on music, lit candles, and poured them each a glass of wine. He let Sadie back inside and whispered into her ear. "Hold a good thought for me, Sadie, that I'm doing the right thing, and please stay out of the way, baby."

Both Christopher and Tyler had their jackets and ties off, and their shirts had the first three or four buttons undone. Tyler put on "Unchained Melody" by Il Divo.

"I've wanted to dance to this Italian version with the perfect man ever since I saw 'Ghost.' Indulge me."

"You never danced it with Ben?"

"No."

The music started, and Tyler put both of his arms around Christopher and buried his face on his chest, taking in the mixed scent of soap, his cologne, and a light sweat. It was intoxicating. Christopher brought Tyler's head up so he could rest his cheek tightly against his and then placed his chin on Tyler's shoulder. He moved his hand up from Tyler's waist and caressed the back of Tyler's head and felt his damp hair. He drank in Tyler's faint scent of Escape and soap from an earlier shower coupled with the dampness that the robust polka had elicited from his body. Christopher was in heaven.

Tyler loved the song "Unchained Melody," and he loved to listen to Italian being spoken even though he didn't speak the language. When he discovered the recording Il Divo made of it in Italian, he felt as if he had just won the trifecta. As the singers' rendition of the words escalated in emotion and volume, he and Christopher instinctively held each other tighter and closer. At last, Tyler felt so safe, so secure, and so loved. He wished this dance would never end. He would just go with it and let the chips fall where they may. That is if they were going to fall at all.

When the song finished, Tyler pulled back from Christopher enough to start to unbutton his shirt completely. He rubbed his hands over Christopher's well defined pecs and kissed each nipple.

Christopher stated, "Tyler, please don't start something you can't finish. Are you certain you want this?"

"I'm sure." Then Tyler kissed his way up Christopher's chest, kissing his Adam's apple, his chin, his cheeks, his nose, his eyelids, his forehead, then back to his full lips. He gently pressed his lips next to Christopher's and just held them there. Christopher pressed his whole body into Tyler's and put his arms around him and returned the kiss. They opened their mouths simultaneously and hungrily welcomed each other's tongue. Savoring the moment, they stood kissing that way in the middle of the living room for the longest time, their bodies swaying slightly in unison to the music. Sadie was on the sofa looking at her master and the man who was so in love with him. She was pleased and went to sleep.

Christopher began to slowly remove Tyler's shirt, all the time kissing him. Tyler stopped long enough to grab Christopher's hand and lead him to the bedroom. During the short journey, they both kicked off their shoes. Once in the bedroom, Tyler turned down the bed, then removed Christopher's socks and dress pants. Christopher started to remove his briefs, but Tyler stopped him. "No, not yet." Christopher was on top of Tyler. Both men were naked except for their underwear. They kissed each other everywhere softly, gently, then roughly, eagerly, hungrily. When Christopher started to suck on Tyler's nipples, Tyler let out a moan. The man had found his "spot." Christopher instinctively knew this and didn't let up. Then they rolled over so that Christopher was on the bottom. Tyler kissed his way down Christopher's body. When he got to his briefs, he took the waistband in his teeth and pulled it back, freeing up Chris's throbbing, huge manhood. With his thumbs on his partner's hips, Tyler deftly removed those briefs that were now in the way of each man's pleasure.

Oh my God! thought Tyler as he started to lick, kiss, caress Christopher's hardness and then engulfed every inch into his warm, wet mouth and throat. It wasn't long before Christopher moaned, "Please stop."

Tyler didn't stop. As if to warn Tyler, Christopher gasped. But Tyler just hunkered down and let this handsome new lover of his know just how much he cared for him. Christopher's whole body shuddered with frenzy as he erupted. Tyler stayed there awhile and then came up and placed his head on Christopher's chest. Christopher would have none of that. He placed his strong hands on Tyler's face, pulled him up to him, and kissed him passionately and deeply. "Now it's my turn."

"Just hold me. It's enough."

"But it isn't enough for me."

He placed Tyler on his back and repeated the whole process with Tyler being the recipient this time. Christopher took his time making sure that Tyler would absolutely know how he felt about him on this level. He made love to every inch of Tyler's body. After Tyler climaxed, Christopher came up next to him and wrapped his big arms around Tyler and whispered, "I love you so much!"

With tears in his eyes, Tyler gently kissed Christopher. Spent, the two men fell asleep holding each other fast.

Sadie came into the room and looked at the lovers asleep in each other's arms, noting that Christopher was on her side of the bed. She jumped up onto the bed and begrudgingly took her new place at the foot of the bed on Tyler's side.

CHAPTER EIGHTEEN

Tyler awoke the next morning to Sadie's whimpering that she needed to go outside. He carefully slipped out of bed so as to not disturb Christopher who was still in a deep slumber. Tyler looked warmly at Christopher, then whispered to Sadie, "Come on, baby. I'll take you outside."

While Sadie ran around the back yard awhile before relieving herself, Tyler contemplated the previous night's events. It had been lustful, passionate, loving, and sensual. *Now what, I wonder? Will Christopher want to see me again? Yes, he said he loved me, but that was in bed. Granted, it was after the fact, not in the heat of passion. Maybe he really does love me. Still, I can't let him know everything about me. Better to save that news for a rainy day, if I do need it. You probably won't, Tyler, because like all newly-gay men, he'll want to start sampling everything in the candy store. You've been down this road before. Why would this time around be any different? It doesn't matter. I have Sadie. Stop thinking about it. You'll give yourself a headache.*

Sadie wanted to stay outside and bask in the sunshine. "I'm going in to shower, Sadie. I'll check back in on you later."

Back in the house, Tyler looked in the bedroom and saw that Christopher was still asleep. Tyler took some clean briefs out of the drawer and went to the bathroom to shower. The warm cascading water felt good on his body, but he didn't linger as long as he might have. He toweled off and quickly dressed. Then he took out a fresh bath towel, wash cloth, and a new toothbrush and placed it on the counter near the lavatory. Since Tyler's dental hygienist gave him a new tooth brush every visit, he always had a couple extra. He went into the bedroom, and Christopher was still asleep. *I'm not letting him sleep all day. I have things to do,* he thought.

Tyler sat on the bed and placing his hand on Christopher's shoulder, shook him a little. "Hey sleepy head. Wake up."

Christopher opened his eyes and smiled, "Good morning." Realizing that Tyler was showered and dressed already, "How long have you been up?"

"About an hour."

"Why didn't you wake me?"

"No need to. Sadie had to go out. I thought I might as well get dressed. There's a towel and a new toothbrush waiting for you in the bathroom. I'll fix us breakfast while you shower."

Tyler went to the kitchen as Christopher headed toward the bathroom. He had already made coffee. *What to make for breakfast?* "I know," he said aloud to himself, "blueberry waffles. And I can cut up that honeydew melon." Tyler got the ingredients from the cupboard and the milk and eggs from the refrigerator, got out a mixing bowl, and started to work. Focused on the task at hand, he hadn't noticed Christopher's entrance into the kitchen.

Christopher walked into the kitchen quietly. Tyler was totally engrossed in pulling a decent breakfast together and hadn't noticed. Christopher came up behind Tyler and put his muscular arms around him, pulling him back from the counter. He buried his face into Tyler's neck and kissed him softly. "I know that you are in the middle of making us a nice breakfast, but please just let me hold you a moment. Indulge me."

Tyler let his body relax back into Christopher's and relished the moment. Then, as if awaking from a deep, beautiful dream, "Mr. Girrardi, you do realize I'm holding a sharp knife, don't you?"

Without saying a word, Christopher put his manly hand over Tyler's and removed the knife. "Now you won't be distracted."

After a few minutes of holding Tyler, Christopher ventured, "I loved every moment of every minute with you last night, and I don't want it to end."

Tyler turned to look into Christopher's eyes. He knew that look. It was the look of someone being in love for the first time. Why is h*e so infatuated with me?* thought Tyler. *Nevertheless, it is nice to hear.*

"Time for breakfast. Do you like waffles?"

Unplugging the heated waffle iron, Christopher whispered into Tyler's ear, "Breakfast can wait." He started to kiss Tyler and took him by the hand and led him back to the bedroom. Christopher let his bath towel drop to the floor. Tyler started to remove his shirt, but Christopher stopped him. "Allow me." In a flash, he had removed Tyler's clothing and gently laid him on the bed. Then Christopher was on top of Tyler, kissing him passionately. Instinctively, Tyler took his right hand and reached into the top drawer of the night stand and took out a new box of Magnum sized condoms and some lube.

"For you."

"How did you know that I would need Magnum size?" Christopher wanted to know.

"You do everything in a big way."

Laughing, Christopher suited up and was soon deep inside Tyler. The new lovers made slow, passionate love and eventually climaxed simultaneously. Spent, they continued to lie in each other's arms, softly stroking and caressing each other.

The spell the new lovers had cast over each other was abruptly broken by Sadie's barking at the back door. "Oh, my God. I forgot I left her outside." He started to get up but Christopher stopped him.

"Before you let her in, first things first. Why, after all of this time, did you finally decide to have sex with me?" Before Tyler could answer, Christopher elaborated. "Let me clarify that statement. Last night was healthy, lustful sex. This morning was making love. What made you change your mind?"

"You reminded me of how much I liked to polka."

"Come on, seriously, why?"

"Last night, I don't know, I saw you in an entirely different light. You awakened something in me. I wanted to be with you."

Christopher smiled and gently kissed Tyler.

The two men got dressed and adjourned to the kitchen. Tyler let a very impatient Sadie back into the house.

"Anything I can do to help?"

"If you would be so kind as to fill Sadie's bowl." Pointing to a door, "Her food is in the pantry. Then if you would put fresh water in her bowl, we would both appreciate it." Tyler finished mixing up the waffle batter. Immediately after pouring some batter on to the hot waffle iron, he added a few fresh blueberries and closed the lid to let it bake. Rinsing off the honeydew melon, he placed it on the cutting board and began to cut it.

"There is some sliced ham in the refrigerator. You can get that out and put some in the microwave to warm up. Then you can pour us each a cup of coffee. There's also some half-and-half in the refrigerator."

After Tyler had poured some dog food in Sadie's bowl, they sat down to breakfast. Christopher started to eat, then stopped when he noticed that Tyler was silent. He was holding his palms upward, one on each side of his plate of food. Then Tyler spoke, "We give thanks to Creator, to the Universe for this meal, for the abundance in our lives, and for the joy and friendship that Christopher and I have. So be it."

"So be it. That was nice. I never say Grace of any kind. I suppose I should."

"That would be up to you. I just know that when I take the time to express gratitude for the abundance in my life, life goes more smoothly. More abundance flows to me. It just does."

"Growing up, we only said Grace on Sunday before dinner. Never at any other meals. I don't know why. Odd that I haven't thought about that in such a long time."

"Eat up before it gets cold."

Hungry, the men ate in relative silence. Following breakfast, Christopher helped Tyler clear the table and put the dirty dishes in the dishwasher. Tyler was impressed with his consideration.

"So, Tyler, what's on your agenda today?"

"I think that I will go for a long walk at the beach. Then sit awhile on my log amidst the beach grass and write in my journal. I haven't done that in awhile. Time to resume that practice." "I've never kept a journal. What kinds of things do you write about?"

"It varies. Whatever is important to me. Today, I'm going to write about this phenomenal date I went on last night."

Taking the bait, Christopher couldn't help but ask, "You went on a date? I thought that you weren't going to date anyone."

"I wasn't, but last night became a date. I would go out with him again. Who knows what's next?

Smiling from ear to ear, Christopher shared, "What a coincidence! I went on a date last night, too. It by far exceeded my expectations."

"He was some lucky guy who went out with you." Tyler paused a moment, then thought, *What the fuck?!* Boldly, he went on, "Do you think that you will see that guy again?"

"God, I hope so! How about you? Will you see your guy again?"

"I don't know. I would like to think that he will call me again soon. I thought things went well, but sometimes you just can't be sure of what the other person is really thinking."

"What would you want to do on your next date with this guy, who by the way, I think would be so lucky to have you in his life?"

"That's easy. I want to go dancing again. Last night, we danced. Oh, how we danced!"

"Dancing. Really?"

"Yeah. I know now how Cinderella must have felt at the ball after she danced with her prince. However, that's a fairy tale of a different sort."

Smiling, Christopher said, "Thank you again for a fantastic evening and breakfast and everything. I should be going."

"Okay. I had a fantastic time as well."

Tyler walked with Christopher to his car. Before he got in, Christopher turned to Tyler, embraced him, and kissed him good-bye.

"The neighbors might be watching, but I don't care."

"We'll talk soon."

"Yes, soon," Tyler replied. Christopher started his car and they waved good bye to each other. As Tyler was walking back into the house, his cell phone rang. It was Christopher.

"Hello," he said as he turned to see that Christopher was still in his driveway on his cell phone.

"Tyler, will you go out with me again? Could we please have another date?"

Tyler was so caught up in the fact that Christopher was so smitten with him. "Just a minute, Christopher. Sorry, but I have to put you on hold. There's a car parked in my driveway." Tyler ran up to Christopher's car. The window was down. Tyler reached in and placed one of his palms on each side of Christopher's face. "Yes, I will go out with you again. Yes! Yes! Yes!"

CHAPTER NINETEEN

Christopher and Tyler began dating on a regular basis. Christopher had never been happier. His secretary, employees, and members of the governing board of directors noticed his seemingly constant state of joy. When they asked him if he was finally seeing someone since his divorce, he answered directly, "Yes, his name is Tyler Reynolds." He let the chips fall where they may. Christopher derived great strength from Tyler's openness about his sexual orientation. Since he was keenly aware the news would eventually get out, he would tell them before they heard it from someone else. One older board member, John Evans, who had been a close friend of Christopher's father, said to him, "Christopher, I really don't understand all of this gay business. No one would have ever suspected you for being one of 'them.' Son, are you truly happy with this lifestyle? I mean, you played football. You were the quarterback!"

"Tyler makes me joyful. I've never been happier since I accepted and embraced my authentic self. I have to do what's right for me."

"Okay, as long as you're happy. I expect if your dad were still here, he might have had a thing or two to say to you about it at the onset, but in the end, all he ever wanted for you was what was best. He wanted you to have someone who loves you with all of her, I mean his, heart. I'd like to meet this Tyler friend of yours."

"You will. I'm taking him to meet mother when she returns from her latest European jaunt. I'll let you know how that goes."

As for Tyler, he was energized at work and was always in a good mood. Whenever Sophie queried him about his relationship with Christopher, he always responded, We're just dating. We're good friends. He confides in me."

"About what?"

"Often he needs to think things through out loud. He'll discuss his work projects, or ideas he has for his company's growth as an example. He appreciates that I can listen without offering any advice. I certainly don't know anything about the corporate world. My listening to what's important to him seems to help him in some way."

"You used to tell me everything about Ben."

"That was different. This," Tyler paused to search for the right word, "this experience with Christopher is unique." Changing the subject, "I wonder how Ben is doing? Is he still married?"

"WHY do you care?"

Tyler didn't respond.

Sophie went on, "The thing about Ben is that he always has a smile. He wants everyone to think that all is well with him and his world. Behind that mask is one lonely man. All one has to do is look into his eyes. The eyes tell all."

Tyler remained silent. He remained focused on the arrangement he was making, wishing that he hadn't brought up Ben's name. Sophie knew him better than anyone; it was true. He still hoped that one day Ben would come to his senses, knock on his door, and tell Tyler that he was ready to be an out and proud gay man. That he had decided it was time to be his authentic self. It was possible. Besides, it was only a matter of time when Christopher would grow tired of Tyler. His current state of affairs with Christopher was too good to last. Or so he kept telling himself. *Sooner or later the other shoe will drop. It's only a matter of time.*

Sophie couldn't resist asking, "So if one day there was a miraculous change in Ben, and he came crawling back to you while you're still dating Christopher, who obviously adores you, you would drop Christopher who is everything Ben isn't. You would drop Christopher and break his heart for Ben?"

"You obviously have been watching too many soap operas.""Don't be a dick, Tyler, I love you dearly. You've been more than a good friend to me, but I would have to have you committed if you made that kind of foolish mistake. Just putting it out there."

"We can't always help who we love. And on that, I think that we should change the subject."

Deep inside, Tyler knew that Sophie was right. As incredibly good and kind that Christopher was to Tyler, Tyler still was holding back. He didn't always give Christopher one-hundred percent like he had to Ben. Occasionally, he wondered if Christopher would ever notice or ever say anything. He seemed to know Tyler pretty well, at least as much as Tyler wanted him to know. The sad truth was that in the past Tyler always gave too much of himself to another man. When it ended, he felt that he had nothing in his inner reserve to draw on. Emotionally bankrupt was perhaps the best way to describe it. He wasn't going to make that same mistake with Christopher.

That weekend, they went for a drive north along the coast of West Michigan. It was unusually warm for this late in the autumn, and Christopher had the top down on the Porsche convertible, his latest acquisition in his car collection. Tyler welcomed the warm breeze blowing on his face. The sunglasses he was wearing were dark enough that Christopher couldn't see into his eyes. The eyes were indeed the windows of the soul, and Tyler really didn't want anyone, especially Christopher, looking there today. He felt a deep melancholy today and didn't know why, only that he didn't want to talk about it or think about it for that matter.

They dined at a restaurant that Christopher had been raving about. Tyler had to admit that the food was fabulously good. The broiled whitefish was excellent. It was getting dark; they headed back south towards home. The fall sky was slowly becoming punctuated with the emerging stars. Suddenly, Christopher turned off of the highway down a dirt road.

"Where are we going?"

"I want to find a quiet place to park, so we can just gaze at the stars."

"Okay." Tyler knew that Christopher's other passion, besides football, was the stars.

They parked in a desolate place. Christopher turned off the engine and just leaned back and stared up at the heavens. Finally, he spoke, "I find this very calming. I feel like I can connect to something bigger than all of us. I guess it must be like when you meditate, from what you've told me."

"This is a form of meditation. One can gaze at a flame, an object, a star, or a constellation and merge with it and listen for what Spirit has to say."

"Sometimes I get lonesome. No, homesick is a better word. It's not like when I'm missing you or my mother. Sometimes, I feel such a deep longing. I look at the stars and I feel connected to my real home."

"That's very cool."

"When I leave the planet, when I go 'home', I will be going back to the stars. That's where I came from."

Tyler looked at Christopher with amazement. "How much do you know about the Star People?"

"A little. Not much. What do you know?"

"Not much. Magda was exploring this topic before she transitioned. Sophie and I still haven't found another teacher who has the integrity that Magda had."

"You don't think I'm crazy?"

"Please, I talk to dead people when I'm giving a reading. Why would I think that you're crazy?"

They laughed. "Let's go home," Christopher said. He put the top up on the car, and they headed back to the main road.

It was late when they got to Christopher's house. Sadie greeted them warmly. Christopher had made a comfortable place in his garage for Sadie when they went away for a few hours. He had a small swinging door put in the wall so that she could go in and out at her leisure. Tyler was amazed at how quickly she adapted to it and didn't seem to mind staying here at all. Sometimes, he wished that he could be as flexible as Sadie was. Sadie was always delighted when they returned.

"Do you want to spend the night with me?" asked Christopher.

"I was hoping to."

They showered together in the huge shower off of the master bedroom and climbed into bed. Christopher reached into the night stand and pulled out a box of condoms.

"Don't you think that we're past using these?" Christopher asked. "We've both been tested and are negative."

"I know. But I just feel better with that protection is all. It's what I'm used to."

"When you marry me, then we won't need these anymore, ever."

"Okay, when we're married."

Tyler knew the condom usage was a deeply ingrained habit from his days of being promiscuous. Ben had never challenged him on it. Looking back, it was probably a good thing since Ben was banging women at the same time as he was Tyler.

Christopher and Tyler made love like never before. For Christopher, it always was like the first time. For Tyler, when

Christopher was on top of him deep inside, it was as if he was transported to another dimension. He had never known such fulfilling passion. *Why can't you just let go of the past and commit your heart 100 percent to him?*

"Oh, my God, Christopher!" Tyler yelled out. Often Tyler liked to get vocal when they were in bed, so Christopher just took this remark as a compliment to his sexual prowess. However, this was not the case this time. For some unknown reason, Tyler suddenly got an incredibly painful spasm in his left foot. It cramped up with intense pain. He knew he would need to stand on it and apply pressure for it to go away. "Christopher, stop! Please. I'm begging you."

"What's wrong?"

"It's my left foot. Please. I need to stand on it now." Tyler hopped out of bed, grabbed the headboard for support and gently put pressure on his left foot. Christopher could see immediately that the foot was in spasm.

"What can I do? Should I get some ice to put on it?"

"No, that's not necessary. Just give me a moment, and it will go away. Shit, what timing. I can't remember the last time this happened. I'm so sorry for ruining the moment."

"Please, no apology is needed." Tyler's foot started to relax and the pain subsided. "Let me massage it."

"No, it's too sore. Let me stand a little longer. I'll be okay."

A few minutes lapsed, and the two men climbed back into bed, and Christopher placed another pillow under Tyler's foot. "It will help it heal if it's elevated, Tyler."

"Thanks."

Tyler, trying to be a good sport about it, said, "I'm really sorry about all of this. We can resume what we were doing if you want to."

"It's late. We can continue our love-making in the morning."

Then, Christopher pulled away slightly so he could look Tyler directly in the eye.

"Tyler, I have been thinking about this for awhile."

"About what?"

"I'm no longer content with the way things are between us. We go places. We have fun. We stay overnight at each other's house now and then."

"What's wrong with that?

"It's not enough for me. I want to give you the world. I want to come home to you every night." Christopher paused, then took Tyler's hands into his and said, "I want to marry you."

Why couldn't things remain the way they were? "It's 2013 but we still can't get married in Michigan."

"I want to get married. You're all I think about. I like being with you. You make me so happy. What say you? Will you please marry me?"

"Married??!! I've never really ever thought about that."

There was an awkward silence, then Tyler broke it. "I mean all I have ever wanted was to have a successful floral business, a comfortable home, and a man who cared about me to share it with. But…."

"But what?

"Christopher, you are generous to a fault. You insist on paying most of the time when we go out. Obviously, I don't have the kind of income you do. I can't spend the kind of money on you that you do on me. I can't afford the expensive hotels and meals at five-star restaurants and orchestra seats at every play and symphony. I don't want to be kept. I have to feel like I'm contributing equally. I can't do that with you if we're married."

"Are you turning me down because I have money, and I want to share it with you? Really? Are you fucking serious?"

"Don't get nasty. I just didn't see this coming. I didn't. I have to think about it is all."

"Wow. Not the answer I expected."

"Christopher, you need someone who is on the same level as you. I don't have the background or the education that you do. I'm not the country-club, golf-course kind of guy. You are." Scrambling for some logic, Tyler continued, "A CEO of a company like yours wouldn't marry a florist. Tongues will wag. You need to marry someone who is a 'somebody.'"

"Since when do you give a shit what other people think? You are a 'somebody,' Tyler." Christopher got out of bed and got on his knees. "Is this better? I'm asking you to be my husband, my partner, my lover, my best friend. Tyler Reynolds, will you marry me?"

"Christopher, you are a knight in shining armour. Please get back into bed." Taking Christopher's hands into his, Tyler went on, "This is a lot for me to process."

"We don't have to get married right away. Would you consider living together in sin for awhile? Then, we'll get married. You and Sadie can move in with me in this big old house that needs your touch."

"We'll talk more. Give me some time. Please." Tyler's mind raced. *This is certainly not how I thought things would go. Because you didn't think at all about where things were going. You're an idiot, Tyler.*

Tyler didn't sleep much that night. The next morning was filled with small talk as Tyler was avoiding the topic of marriage. After breakfast, Tyler said, "I need to go home and rake some leaves and do some yard work. What are you doing today?"

"Probably watch football." Firmly and with all the resolve he could muster, "I'm going to say this one more time, Tyler. In case you haven't noticed, I love you. I have loved you since the first time I laid eyes on you at Carmella's party. I want us to live together. I want to marry you. I want you to be my life-partner and my husband. Take some time to think about it, and let me know. I deserve an answer."

Tyler nodded his head, "Yes, you do. That's only fair."

They kissed good-bye and Tyler and Sadie drove away.

Who was the wise sage who had once said, "Be careful for what you ask for because you may get it.

CHAPTER TWENTY

A week went by, and Tyler didn't see Christopher or get a phone call. Occasionally, he received a text message: "Thinking of you" or "Hope you're having a good day, very busy here." That was it. It felt so unusual to Tyler since in the past, Christopher had always called to tell him those same messages. Even if Tyler was busy and couldn't answer and it went to voice mail, Christopher would leave a message. Granted, when Tyler made the decision to have sex with Christopher, he told himself that Christopher would soon tire of him and move on. That hadn't happened. He had to admit to himself that he missed hearing Christopher's voice. It always made his heart smile to hear Christopher say that he was thinking of him. Maybe he had been taking Christopher for granted all this time. That certainly was not his intention. *Perhaps you really are self-centered. You have allowed yourself to get carried away with Christopher. Did you honestly think that could not happen? You can't control things like you thought you could, can you?* Tyler knew that he absolutely could not accept Christopher's marriage offer. If they did get married, he didn't want Christopher to ever find out about his past. There was nothing he could do to change it. He certainly didn't want it to come up later and have it revealed. It needed to remain the dark, ugly, hidden secret it was. *Why couldn't they just go on with things the way they were? That would be too easy.* Why wasn't Christopher content with the status quo? Whenever Tyler mulled all of this over, he became overwhelmed and forced himself to to think of something else.

Sophie's question brought him back to the present. "Have you heard from Christopher this week? He usually pops in or calls you while we're here at work. Is he around this week, or has work taken him out of town?"

"I don't know. I guess he's busy," was his lame reply.

"Ummmm, yes you do know, Tyler. Don't bullshit me. I can tell by your voice something is up. Did you two have an argument?"

"No, no argument."

"Then what is it? You haven't mentioned him lately. What's up?"

"Christopher wants to take the relationship another step further. I don't know that I can do that."

"Further in what way?"

After a long pause and in a a somber voice came the answer. "He asked me to marry him."

"That's wonderful! You said 'yes,' didn't you?"

"I told him I had to think about it."

"THINK about it? Think about what?" Sophie was having trouble wrapping her mind around Tyler's response. "The man adores you. He dotes on you, would do anything for you. He's kind, patient, has a great sense of humor. You enjoy each other's company. I know you do. You would never have to worry about money again."

"I don't worry about money now. I can always manage that."

"Are you're still carrying a torch for Ben?"

There was no answer from Tyler.

"Well, are you? Because if you are, from where I stand, that is ridiculous. Even if Ben suddenly came back into your life, which is NOT going to happen, Ben Thompson is not the man Christopher Girrardi is. There is no comparison. Ben never treated you with the respect that Christopher does. Why didn't you say YES? I don't get it."

Tyler looked at Sophie blankly.

"Did it ever occur to you that Ben wasn't in the same relationship with you that you were with him? Think about that."

Meekly and struggling to admit that Sophie was correct, he admitted, "You are so right. I feel so incredibly fucked up inside. You know me well, yet there are a couple things you don't know about me. Things I don't have the courage to talk about. I just can't." Tyler paused, "There you have it."

"Okay. If you need to fill me in on whatever it is that I don't know, I'm a good listener." Giving Tyler a bear hug, "I'm always here for you."

"Thank you."

And so it went for another ten days. Whenever Tyler called Christopher, the message went to voice mail. Tyler would text him as well with general messages: "Thinking of you, hoping you are having a great day, too." The text response was always the same: "Tell me when you have reached a decision. Then we will meet, and you can tell me that decision to my face. Until then, I will give you some space to think clearly. Hugs, Chris."

It was nearly two weeks later when Tyler took Sophie out for dinner on a Wednesday evening to celebrate her birthday. They went to Patty's, a favorite of theirs, and were enjoying wine with dinner. Patty's always had an interesting and varied clientele. They both enjoyed people-watching as well as the fabulous Italian cuisine. As they finished up their crème brulee Sophie glanced across the restaurant. "Oh my God. There's Christopher with a man in the far booth in the opposite corner. I never saw them come in."

Tyler turned to look at his boyfriend who, it seemed to him, was being all-too-friendly with the athletic, debonair blond man sitting across from Christopher. He appeared to be about Christopher's age and could easily have passed for Robert Redford's twin brother when he was of that age.

"They appear to be having a very good time, don't they."

Tyler watched them intently. They were incredibly engrossed with each other's company. Tyler could not explain where the pangs of jealously came from that suddenly filled his body, his mind, and his heart. *What's this you're feeling now, Tyler? You always told yourself that Christopher would tire of you and move on.*

Sophie, always the shrewd observer said, "What is that ring, which looks like a wedding band, on his ring finger? I've never seen him wear any rings since he's been dating you."

Tyler was dumbfounded.

The Robert Redford clone then reached across the table, took Christopher's hand in his, and said something. Christopher placed his free hand on his dinner companion's hand and smiling, answered. *God, do I wish I could read lips right now!*

"It certainly didn't take him long to find someone else."

"Tyler, you don't know what that is all about."

What bothered Tyler the most were the looks that Christopher was giving the guy. Tyler knew those glances. He had been the recipient many times. Often, when they were together, Tyler would gaze up and see how Christopher was staring at him lovingly. It wasn't that long ago that Christopher made that direct eye contact with him when he had proposed.

"I think I do. He used to look at me that way when he was wooing me." Tyler downed the rest of his wine. A few minutes earlier, he thought he didn't need to finish it before driving home. Now driving was the last thing on his mind.

"There was obviously a good reason I waited to give him an answer. He's just made it so much easier for me tell him."

"You don't think that you're jumping to conclusions?"

"No, I don't. Come on, Sophie, let's go. But first I want Christopher to know that we're here, and I have reached a decision."

"Oh, Tyler, not here." This was not going to be pretty.

Tyler walked directly across the room to the booth where Christopher and the fair-haired man were seated. They were still laughing and having a marvelous time.

"Christopher, so good to see you out and about."

"Tyler, Sophie, I didn't see you here."

"Obviously."

Christopher started to introduce his dinner companion,"Tyler, Sophie, I want you to meet---"

Cutting him off, Tyler started in, "I don't need to know his fucking name, Christopher. I don't care. If it wasn't him, I'm sure it would be someone else."

"Hey bud, you've got it all wrong. Christopher—"

Directing his anger to the Robert Redford look-alike, "I am not talking to you. Here's a thought, just shut the fuck up!"

"Tyler, stop it."

"You shut the fuck up, too, Christopher. Maybe I didn't tell you what you wanted to hear right away about getting married, and listening to your 'you can't live without me and all of that shit,' you found someone else to fill the gap. You're SO efficient. You certainly didn't waste any time. Or, has this been going on for some time? Maybe when you had to go out of town on business?"

"Lower your voice. This is not the place."

"It's as good as any." Tyler turned to leave, then abruptly turned back. "Oh, and by the way, Christopher, NO, I DO NOT WANT TO MARRY YOU. I DON'T WANT TO EVER HEAR FROM YOU OR SEE YOU AGAIN." To the blond man, "Good luck, bucco, Mr. Girrardi is all yours."

With that, Tyler stormed out of the restaurant with Sophie at his heels. Tyler was too angry to unlock his car door when he felt a hand on his shoulder spin him around. It was Christopher, and he was pissed. Tyler had never seen him so angry. For the first time, he was a little frightened of the former quarterback.

"Who the fuck do you think you are, making a scene like that in a public place? I have never been so humiliated, so embarrassed in my life."

"Just telling the truth."

"You're drunk."

"I wish I was, but I'm not."

"Oh, so this tantrum of yours is all about the truth, huh? You don't know a damn thing about my friend or our past. We are good friends. I've known Alec since high school. He was in town and wanted to have dinner and catch up. I was telling him all about you and what a great guy you are. How wonderful I *thought you were*."

"Yeah? I don't buy it."

"You couldn't give me an answer, Tyler, when I asked you to marry me. You expect me to sit at home and twiddle my thumbs for God knows how long until you get your shit together enough to give me a response?"

"Yes."

"You arrogant prick. This evening I have seen a side to you that I have never seen before, and I don't like it at all. You can forget I ever asked you to marry me. You and I are finished, Mr. Reynolds."

"Why are you wearing a wedding band, Christopher? Explain that."

"I obviously prematurely bought us rings. I was showing them to Alec. Don't worry, I'll return them!"

"You're always paying for everything! You just went out and bought rings. I don't have a say in that matter because I'm not wealthy like you are. Jesus, Christopher. You're too much!"

Christopher turned to go, then stopped and turned back. "And just for the record, that outburst of yours was very incongruous with the alleged spiritual path that you're supposedly on. I do know that much."

Christopher went back inside the restaurant. Sophie and Tyler got inside the car. Tyler stared at the dashboard before saying anything. "I'm really sorry about ruining your birthday dinner with my shit."

"Dinner was nice up until you saw Christopher. You really think that he is sleeping with that guy?"

"Yes, I do. It had to end anyway. What's the difference how? Might as well end this way. It is what it is. And that's the end of all of that."

Sophie didn't say a word, but she knew as well as Tyler did, that this was not the end of "all that."

CHAPTER TWENTY ONE

Two weeks went by, then three. On one hand, Tyler really thought that eventually he would have heard something from Christopher. *Why would you? He told you quite emphatically that he was finished with you. You also thought that Ben would come around, too. It's not in the cards, Tyler. Not with the men you have attracted into your life.*

Most of the time, Tyler could convince himself that his relationship with Christopher had to end at some point anyway. No matter how hard he tried to forget about the past, he knew it would have reared its ugly head. No, it was better this way. But this pain was different than when Ben left him for a woman. When Ben left, Tyler went on an eating binge, calling everything comfort food. He tried it this time but found that most of the time he couldn't eat. He lost fifteen pounds in two-and-a-half weeks. Tyler had always loved to cook, but food didn't interest him anymore. When he did take the time and effort to fix something appetizing, he usually ended up tossing it in the garbage. *I needed to lose weight anyway,* he thought. Still, the pain was different. Why was that? Maybe all men were just assholes one way or another. *Maybe you're the asshole, Tyler.* Magda had told him not to "fuck this up." *Well, I didn't fuck it up. I caught him with someone else after all he said about loving me and wanting to marry me and all that crap. Yup. It was just all crap.*

Mulling all of this over and over most of the time, since that is all he could think of, put him in a low vibration, emotionally speaking. He had been reading about Law of Attraction since the blowup with Christopher. Law of Attraction says in order to manifest what you want, it is accomplished by trying to be on a higher vibrational level. Being distraught because your boyfriend was obviously seeing a good looking man, who probably had a lot more to offer, was not conducive. Screw it. No man was worth feeling like this.

Tyler walked into the kitchen to pour himself another cup of coffee. On the counter, next to the coffee pot was a huge sweet onion that he hadn't put away. He picked up the onion and slowly started to peel it. Though not as strong as a yellow cooking onion, the sweet onion still brought tears to his eyes when he stripped away the layers. As he pulled away each layer, Tyler examined the texture closely. *The center has the same effect on me as the first layer. Still, it's good to look at what's inside of us. Maybe then we can start to change, even if the onion is the same at its core.* Gradually the onion had been totally dismantled and was in pieces on the counter top. *Forgive yourself, Tyler, for kidding yourself into thinking that life with Christopher would be the never ending fairy tale. Forgive yourself for thinking you could have it all. Put it behind you.* But to put it behind him Tyler realized that the self-forgiveness would have to start with an apology to Christopher. Whether Christopher was seeing someone else or not didn't justify Tyler's behavior at Patty's that night. It was all so much easier said than done.

It was on Monday going into the fourth week that Tyler put a little more effort into his appearance when getting ready for work. He wore his black jeans and a white patterned linen shirt. If the store wasn't too busy, he'd ask Sophie to cover for him. He would go to Christopher's office, try to get in to see him and apologize for making a scene and embarrassing him in public. He didn't want his last words to Christopher to be harsh ones.

Sophie knew something was up. "Business appointment? You're looking sharp today. Didn't Christopher give you that shirt?"

"Yes, he did. If you must know, I'm going to go to his office. Maybe he will see me, maybe he won't. If not, I will sit and wait until he emerges from his office. I'm going to apologize for my rude behavior."

Tyler had arranged a dozen white roses in a vase as a peace offering. "I'll give him these, say I'm sorry, and leave. That will be that, and then I can put all of this ugliness behind me and move on."

"I'm glad that you're finally doing this. Take as much time as you need." Sophie hugged Tyler as he left.

Tyler became increasingly nervous as he approached Christopher's corporate offices. When he arrived at the office door, he took his handkerchief out of his pocket and wiped the nervous perspiration from his forehead. *Why am I perspiring?* he asked himself. *I sweat when I'm onstage performing, and I hate that, too. This is not a performance. This is real. Who are you kidding, Tyler? You need to put your feelings for this man aside, apologize for your behavior, and leave. Don't wait for him to say anything. Just get the words out and leave.*

Tyler parked in the visitor's section near the main entrance of Girrardi and Associates, Inc. The grounds and the building which housed the corporate offices of the successful marketing firm was impressive. Summoning his courage, Tyler walked confidently into the lobby of the main office and approached the receptionist. He asked if he could see Mr. Girrardi.

Looking at her computer screen, "Sir, do you have an appointment?"

"No. Please tell him Tyler Reynolds is here to see him. All I need is three minutes of his time."

"If it is to deliver those flowers, I will see that he gets them, Mr. Reynolds."

"Thank you, but I will deliver them myself."

The receptionist picked up her phone and dialed Christopher's extension. "There is a Mr. Tyler Reynolds here to see you." The receptionist paused, looked up at Tyler and politely said, "Yes, I will."

Hanging up the phone, she offered, "Mr. Girrardi is very busy today and can't be interrupted. He requested that you make an appointment to see him on another day."

Fuck, thought Tyler. I*t took all of my courage to come here today.*

"I'll just wait if you don't mind. I only need a minute of his time." Tyler knew that eventually Christopher would have to come out of his office for lunch or something.

Tyler sat down and waited. Fifteen minutes, a half-hour, then an hour went by. He pretended to read a magazine to pass the time, but he couldn't stay focused on the article. It was on the role that business played in the economy, but he found it rather boring. Maybe he should have tried to read this earlier and discussed it with Christopher who would have totally understood it and explained the parts that he didn't get. Too late for that now. He didn't really pay attention to what the secretary was doing and wasn't sure if she was talking about him when an inside call came to her. "Yes, sir. He is."

After an hour-and-a-half, Tyler thought that he would be there all day. Suddenly, the door opened to Christopher's office. He emerged and looked at Tyler. Christopher had no expression on his face.

"Tyler, do you really need to see me? I'm very busy today."

"Please, Christopher. Just give me three minutes of your time. I swear that's all."

Christopher motioned Tyler into his office. Tyler walked past Christopher into his office. He had been here once before. It was on a Saturday and Christopher needed to run in and get a report that he was working on and wanted to finish at home. That had been a congenial time. Today the air was filled with tension. Still Tyler looked around at the dark-cherry wood paneling, the huge cherry desk, the rich leather chair behind it. There were two leather chairs facing Christopher's desk, and there was a brown leather couch against one wall. It was very well-decorated, with masculinity oozing out of everything in it. Christopher closed the door behind them. "Have a seat," he said, pointing to either of the two chairs across from where he sat.

"Thank you, but I'd prefer to stand. In old western movies, when there was fighting, one side would hold up a white flag to declare a truce. I don't have a white flag. All I have are these white roses to offer you."

Tyler extended the vase to Christopher. "You can set them on that table. Thank you."

As Tyler carefully set the flowers on the table between and Christopher and him he said, "I want to apologize to you and to your dinner companion. Hopefully, you can pass this apology along to him. I want to apologize for my rude behavior and crude remarks to you at Patty's several weeks ago. You certainly are free to have dinner with anyone you choose to do so. It's just that...."

"Tyler—"

"No, please let me finish. You don't have to say anything. I am not asking for your forgiveness. I don't expect that, and I don't deserve it either. I guess I cared for you so much more than I ever thought I would. I lashed out when I saw what I perceived as you being with someone for a romantic evening. Which is your right, since I hadn't given you an answer to your marriage proposal and since we hadn't ever really talked about being monogamous with each other. I thought that was understood. But regardless, that was no excuse for me coming unglued when I saw you look into his eyes and hold his hand the way you always held mine when you told me you loved me." Tyler paused to take a breath and plunged on. "I'm really grateful for the time we had together. However, the truth is you deserve better than what I can offer you. Please accept these white roses as my peace offering. Thanks for listening to me. I need to go. I'm sure that I have used up more than the three minutes I asked for."

Tyler turned quickly away and headed toward the door.

"Stop right there. Please, stop. I have missed you so much these past weeks, but my pride wouldn't let me contact you. For awhile, I was so incredibly angry with you."

"I don't blame you. However, you must have someone new now. And good for you. You need to be happy."

"Just like that? You think I already have someone new? You don't know me at all. That's not me."

Tyler knew it wasn't. "No, it's not."

"Alec is an old acquaintance of mine. He was my first love. We've known each other since high school. We roomed together in college. We were best buds. During my senior year we slept together. The next day, filled with disgust, he told me he wasn't 'like that' and that our friendship was over. He hasn't spoken to me since then. I was devastated. I loved him terribly. He's the only man I ever felt anything for until I met you."

"You looked like you were getting along quite well."

"He contacted me a couple of weeks ago, was going to be in town. Could we meet for a drink and dinner? I said yes."

"He appeared to be doing well. He looked successful in life."

"Success isn't just about money, Tyler, as you well know. He's married with kids, makes lots of money. Long story short, he has 'that itch' and wanted to fool around with me again. And couldn't we be 'down low friends with benefits'?"

"Well, he must have just realized how incredibly awesome you are."

"I told him that I didn't want that. I don't ever want to be someone's 'friend with benefits' who sneaks around on his wife."

"I told him about you, about us, how much I loved you. Then you came up to the table, and the rest is history."

"Oh. Well." Tyler was at a loss. He felt like a nickel waiting for change.

"What is it about you that I don't know? What are you not telling me?"

"Christopher, you come from a stable family. You were loved all through your childhood by loving parents. You were given the best of everything--education, a home, culture, and the best that money can buy, and you have all of that in addition to being incredibly handsome, and you possess a winning personality. You deserve the best partner you can find. I'm not it."

"Okay, we have had two very different childhoods. Who hasn't?"

Tyler paused and looked down at the floor. "I have a past."

"Who doesn't?"

"You came riding into my life like a knight in shining armor on a white steed. If you were looking for someone to rescue, I guess you thought I would do. I am white trash, one step removed. I grew up on the wrong side of the tracks. Every opportunity you had given to you, I didn't."

"I don't care about that. God, I wish that you could see yourself the way I see you."

"As what?"

"Sometimes you try to be so tough. You put up walls. You've put one up with us now. Behind that wall is a loving man that I still care about." Christopher paused as Tyler looked away. "You have worked so hard to make something of yourself. You have a good business, you're talented. I've seen you onstage at the theater. You're witty. You're handsome."

"I'm not. Stop with that."

"Please don't interrupt me, and please don't insult me by implying that I can't recognize admirable traits in you. You've helped me be the man I need to be. I looked at you and thought, 'That guy is gay, doesn't give a shit what people think, and lives proudly.' You gave me the inspiration to be me, to come out and be a proud gay man, too."

"Thank you, but you would have done that anyway. It just might have taken you a little longer is all."

"I don't want to lose you."

"Christopher, you're making this very hard for me." With tears in his eyes and looking everywhere except at Christopher's face, Tyler let the flood gates down and spilled everything. "I have a past, something that no one knows about. I can't marry you. You deserve better."

"I'm not following this."

"I have a sordid past that you know nothing about. You're a somebody in the community. You're good and kind and loving and trusting. I'm not." Tyler paused to take a breath. "My mother threw me out of the house at sixteen. I had no money. I hitch hiked to Chicago. I sold myself to survive. I was a cheap whore for money. Oh, I'm just doing it to pay the rent or to get something to eat, is what I told myself. Then it became a way of life. You have no idea the things that I have done for money."

"Try me."

"Jesus." Looking down at the floor Tyler continued, "I have literally let men do very degrading things to me for cash. I am so ashamed to tell you specifics. I have been tied up and beaten. I have tied men up and beat them. I've been the dominatrix wearing stiletto heels and walking on their chests carrying a whip. I've let men call me filthy names while they did sordid things."

"Like what?"

Shaking his head, "I can't tell you. Please don't make me tell you. It's too vile. At first, I did it just to survive. Then I thought, well, I can do this because it's not really me. I'll be a character. I'll pretend that it's somebody else that is the recipient of their words and actions. It's not really happening to me. And then one day, I thought, who are you kidding, Tyler? You have no self-esteem to let anybody treat you like this. It's not about the money. So, I thought that they could just pay me money and talk nicely to me, but nobody wanted that because I was just some dumb whore who couldn't get a real job that paid anything. I didn't know what to do or where to turn. I didn't have any kind of a belief system in those days. Nevertheless, I got down on my knees one day and asked God, if He existed, to show me a way out. Because I really didn't want to live any longer. Later that day I met Hank. Hank never laid a hand on me. He gave me a place to stay, taught me the flower business, and taught me to believe in myself for the first time. Hank saved my life. He helped me find my inner Light. He really was an angel sent to help me." Now that it was all out, Tyler resigned, finished with, "Now, Christopher, you know what I have never wanted you to know."

"Oh, Tyler."

Sobbing now, Tyler went on, "No one has ever loved me like you have. I just wanted things to go along the way they were, but I should have known better. Nothing stays the same. Then you wanted to get married. I thought if I married you and didn't tell you about that part of my life, you would find out about it eventually and hate me, despise me, and kick me out of your life. That night at Patty's, I thought on some level, I'd found an excuse to end things, and you wouldn't have to know about my past. But now you do know."

There was a long silence. Tyler couldn't bring himself to look at Christopher. Finally when Tyler did look up at him, tears were rolling down Christopher's face. Christopher walked over to Tyler, took him into his arms, and just held him.

"I'm here for you, Tyler. I am so here for you."

Tyler let loose with more tears and sobbed against Christopher's chest. When Tyler's crying subsided, Christopher pulled back from Tyler and slowly kissed him on his Third Eye area. "Is there anything else I need to know? Because if there is, I want to hear it now so we can be done with it and move on."

"No, that's pretty much it."

"Are you sure? There is nothing else that you've been hiding from me?"

Trying to smile and with tear-stained cheeks, "Other than the fact that I really don't like sushi, no."

"Your past and sushi, that's it?" Christopher was smiling at Tyler.

"Yes."

"Good," Christopher said, taking his handkerchief and drying Tyler's face, "because you are getting salt water on my silk tie."

"Sorry."

"Tyler, do you think that it would be possible for us to put all of this unpleasantness behind us? Do you think that, together, we could move forward from this point?"

"Really? Seriously? You want to do that with me?"

"Yes, seriously. I do."

"Were you by chance a consultant for the movie *Pretty Woman*? Shaking his head, "No. Were you?"

"I'd like to start again, Christopher, if you want to."

"I do. I also have work to do now, Tyler, and I think that Sophie will be wondering what took you so long. Would it be okay if I came by tonight and we went somewhere and had dinner? We'll talk more."

"Okay. I'd like that very much."

They embraced each other, and Tyler left Christopher's office. *That certainly didn't go the way I anticipated,* Tyler thought. *But what has?*

CHAPTER TWENTY TWO

Christopher showed up at exactly 6:30 with a bottle of cabernet sauvignon in hand. You could set a clock based on his punctuality. "I thought perhaps we could have a glass of wine before going out to eat," he offered.

"If it's okay with you, we can eat here. There is a pizza in the oven and I made a caesar salad."

"Did you by chance make that pizza?"

"Yes, sir, I did. With everything on it that you like, including anchovies."

Grinning, Christopher came back with, "If I didn't know you better, I'd say that you're trying to get on my good side."

"Is it that obvious? For the record, a good side is the only side you have."

Smiling, "You noticed."

"Open the wine, please, and I'll check on the pizza."

They dined and made small talk, and it seemed like old times to both of them. After dinner, they moved to the sofa in the living room. Tyler brought coffee in and set the mugs on the coffee table. "Would you like an after-dinner liqueur, sir?"

"What do you have?"

"There is B & B, amaretto, kahlua or Franjelico."

"Benedictine and Brandy would be fine."

Tyler poured B & B into a snifter for Christopher and amaretto into a snifter for himself. Tyler prided himself on having some decent stemware he'd found long ago at an estate sale. In fact, most of his furnishings were from both estate sales and high-end yard sales.

Tyler handed a snifter to Christopher. "To a new beginning." Christopher looked at Tyler affectionately.

"To a new beginning." They clinked glasses and sipped the liqueur.

"Thank you for being the magnanimous man you are." Tyler settled in next to Christopher on the sofa. Sadie took her place at his feet. Christopher put his strong hand on Tyler's. "So, Tyler Reynolds, where do we go from here?"

"Gaily forward, hopefully."

"Then let's agree, if you want to know anything about me, whom I'm with, or whatever, then I expect you to ask me. Do not let it fester inside until you explode. That isn't good for either of us. Anything that you want to know, ask me, Tyler. I have nothing to hide. Seriously."

"Okay. I will. And do the same to me. Ask me anything. No more secrets. I absolutely hated how I felt when all of that poison surfaced. I guess I thought on some silly level, that if I hurt or embarrassed you, I would be the one in control of leaving this time. I thought it wouldn't hurt if I initiated ending things. It was stupid."

"Yes, hindsight is always twenty/twenty."

"Tell me how you felt. And if there are times I don't ask, tell me anyway."

"Shocked, angered, very hurt."

Taking Christopher's hand and kissing the back of it, "I'm so sorry. Not only was I not walking on the Red Road, I was in the ditch."

Kissing Tyler on the forehead, "It's behind us now."

"You make me want to be a better person, Christopher."

"There is so much that we can learn from each other, and we can love each other in the process." Christopher took Tyler's hands in his and looked him directly into his hazel eyes. "Come closer, Tyler. I just want to hold you and be held by you."

They became one on the sofa, arms and legs intertwined, faces buried in each others' necks. "God, I missed you, missed this. I love cuddling with you."

The two lovers embraced for the longest time, being in the moment with each other. Finally, Christopher broke the embrace and said, "It's getting late, and I have an early-morning appointment. I need to go."

"I know. Morning comes early for both of us."

"You know if you married me, neither one of us would have to leave to go home. I'm asking you again, Tyler. Please marry me. You and Sadie should move in with me. You can redecorate if you want to. You can make one of the spare bedrooms into your meditation room, and another bedroom for an office or whatever. You will have your space separate from mine. That way we won't smother each other. What do you say?"

"Christopher Girrardi, I accept your proposal on one condition."

"And that would be what?"

"Let's date awhile longer, then I'll move in with you. Don't you think perhaps we could live together in sin? Besides, we still can't get married in Michigan."

"I thought you didn't believe in the concept of 'sin.' That to sin really meant 'to miss the mark.'"

"It does. You and I have already had practice in missing the mark. It just sounds kind of deliciously naughty to say we're going to live together in sin."

Laughing, "It does. I want you to meet my mother soon. You'll like her, I know."

"Let me know when."

"I'll check with her and her schedule. Next weekend perhaps. Okay?"

"Yes."

"Good night, sweetheart." Christopher kissed Tyler passionately and then left.

As Christopher drove away, Tyler turned off the porch light. "Sadie, we're going to be moving. He must have been a knight-in-shining-armor in a previous life time."

CHAPTER TWENTY THREE

Things were moving along ever so quickly since Christopher and Tyler reconciled. It was a good feeling, and Tyler certainly didn't have regrets about the direction that his life was heading.

It was Saturday morning, and Christopher had spent the night at Tyler's. Prior to getting ready for the hour drive to meet Doris, Christopher's mother, the lovers went for a jog in the park.

The morning air was crisp enough to see one's breath. While walking near the softball field, Tyler noticed the son of one of his clients. Little Jimmy Rogers was obviously with his dad for the weekend. Mr. Rogers, who was an outstanding athlete in his youth, was pitching balls to Jimmy. Try as he might, Jimmy just couldn't get the bat to make contact with the ball. The more frustrated Jimmy got at his lack of athletic ability, the more his father yelled at him. Tyler wondered why parents thought yelling at their kids during sports would make them better athletes.

"Hey, Jimmy!" Tyler called out. "How's it going?" Tyler jogged over to intervene if he could. Christopher hung back, within earshot.

"Hi, Tyler. Dad, this is Tyler. He owns the shop where Mom gets her flowers."

"Hi," was all the surly man could get out of his mouth.

"Jimmy. I noticed that you and your dad are playing ball. I just wanted to tell you a trick I used when I was your age. When your dad pitches the ball to you, keep your eye on it. But in your mind's eye," Tyler tapped his forehead to illustrate, "I want you to visualize this bat making hard contact with that ball so you are going to send that ball into outer space. Want to try it? If it doesn't work the first time, then just keep practicing it. Visualize success. I know that you can do it!"

"Thanks, Tyler. I'll try it."

Muttering, Jimmy's father then said, "Looks like your jogging partner is waiting for you."

Jimmy's father pitched another ball to his son. Jimmy swung and missed it. Jimmy retrieved the ball and tossed it back to his dad. Jimmy looked at Tyler who mouthed the words: "You can do it." While touching his third eye, Tyler gave Jimmy a thumb's-up signal. Mr. Rogers pitched another ball. Jimmy swung, hitting the ball far into the outfield. Had it been a real game, it would have been a home-run. "Way to go, Jimmy!" Mr. Rogers didn't know what to think.

Tyler rejoined Christopher for their jog. He looked at Tyler with a renewed admiration.

"What?" Tyler asked. "I just did what I wish someone would have done for me in that situation. Race you home."

They began the drive to Doris Girrardi's home outside Ludington. "What have you told your mother about me?"

Christopher gave Tyler an account of what transpired. He'd had a heart-to-heart talk with her a week before their falling out at Patty's restaurant. Although it wasn't the easiest conversation for Christopher to have, he always had an open and honest relationship with his parents. He was buoyed by the fact that his mother always said, "Life is a journey, and we have to make the best of any road that we happen to find ourselves on." Besides, he learned as a teenager not to try to hide anything from Mom or Dad. If he did do something he shouldn't have and they found out about it, he got a tongue-lashing from them about being honest though it might be difficult. They would always end the discussion with, "I'm so disappointed with your sense of judgment, with the fact that you didn't think that you could tell us this." The look on their faces was worse than any physical punishment they could have handed out. On that day, Christopher reminded Doris, "Mom, you always wanted me to be upfront with you. I am doing that today. You know my marriage to Karen was never quite right." And she said, "Yes, and if you recall, I told you on the morning of your wedding day that you didn't have to proceed with that if you weren't one-hundred-percent SURE it was the right thing to do." He told her he remembered, but he had wanted to believe it had been the right thing to do. "Mom, I have met a wonderful man named Tyler. I've known him for about a year. We've been seeing each other exclusively for about six months. I'm head-over-heels in love with him. And then she said while taking my hands into hers, 'This isn't the kind of life I envisioned for you. But I have to say the thought that you might be gay did cross my mind as you went through high school and college when you were never girl-crazy as your friends were. Actually, I was relieved you didn't knock up a girl like your friend, Alec Stanton did. Then later you met and married Karen. I never thought she was right for you for lots of reasons.' Christopher's mother had been silent for a few beats. "The bottom line, Chris, is are you happy?"

"Yes," I told her.

"That's all that matters."

Tyler breathed a sigh of relief. Hopefully this meeting would go smoothly.

Christopher continued on about how good she thought he looked since the divorce. "Then my mother took my hand and said, 'Tell me all about him. Tyler, is it? When can I meet him?'"

"In a few weeks when we coordinate our schedules. You can see for yourself."

That's how it went. Christopher was as relieved as was Tyler.

Tyler was proud of Christopher for being so upfront with his mother. But this was Christopher. Tyler was coming to expect nothing less from his boyfriend. "You must have a great relationship."

"We do. And you will, too."

The navy blue BMW pulled into the driveway of Doris' two-story brick home with a three-car attached garage. It was late autumn. A few stubborn leaves clung to the branches. Although her home was not as large as Christopher's, it seemed too large to Tyler for one person. "You grew up in this house?"

"No," Chris replied. Mother moved here several years ago when she decided to downsize."

"Downsize?"

"Yes. I grew up in a huge house with maid's quarters."

"I see."

Tyler had brought a gorgeous arrangement of fall flowers featuring red and golden yellow mums as a gift. He wanted to give Doris something. It would serve as a great ice-breaker, if needed.

Parking the car in the circle drive by the front entrance, Christopher announced, "Come on, time to meet Mother."

Doris opened the front door while the boys walked up the steps. "Christopher! Let me look at you."

"Mother, it hasn't been that long. A few weeks is all."

"I know. But it is always good to see my boy." Doris embraced him, and Christopher kissed her on the cheek. "You must be Tyler. Christopher, you didn't tell me he was so handsome."

Blushing slightly, "Mrs. Girrardi, I'm so happy to finally meet you. Christopher has told me so much about you. I must say you did a fantastic job of raising him." Tyler wasn't sure what to expect, but Doris Girrardi certainly looked a lot younger than the seventy-year-old Christopher had described. She was trim at 5'5." Obviously she exercised on a regular basis. Her red hair and enthusiasm reminded Tyler of Shirley Maclaine, at least what he knew of Shirley MacLaine at that age.

Entering the house, Tyler noticed the marble floor in the foyer. Lots of artwork hung on the walls. *Doris must be a collector,* he thought.

"Let's go in to the living room. Would you like something to drink? Iced tea, lemonade, something stronger? I suppose it is too early to have martinis."

"Tyler pretty much sticks to wine Mother, but we can have a martini if you want. Then we can go have lunch."

"We'll lunch here. My housekeeper and right hand, Maria, has made manicotti for us." Turing toward Tyler, "Do you like manicotti?"

"I love it."

"Chris, would you mind being our bartender?" Doris motioned toward the bar, "I'll have a martini, two olives, and use the Grey Goose, please. Tyler, red or white wine? I have both."

"I'll join you in a martini, Mrs. Girrardi. But Christopher, go lightly on the gin, please."

"An easy order," the smiling bartender acknowledged.

"Tyler, sit by me. I want to get to know you. Chris speaks highly of you. Later, I'll give you the grand tour of the house and gardens. Maybe you can help me with my azaleas. Chris says you know a lot about flowers."

"I'm a florist. I have my own shop. Although I'm a big fan of beautiful landscaping, I don't know as much about designing it. I would enjoy seeing your gardens."

"I'll show you after lunch. First things, first. How did you two meet?"

"Mother, I told you all that."

"I know. But I want to see if you left anything out." Smiling, Doris turned to Tyler, "So, tell me."

Tyler gave Doris the *Reader's Digest* version. He quickly recounted seeing Christopher at Carmella's party, then he stopped briefly into the shop with his then-wife. Later, he saw him while jogging on the beach where Tyler was meditating. A few days later, Christopher stopped in and ended up delivering flowers for him that afternoon. "I was just out of a relationship and really wasn't interested in dating anyone. I told Christopher that, but he was very persistent. Eventually I gave in to his charm. Now, months later, here we are."

"That's precisely what Chris told me. I thought he might have inadvertently omitted something," Doris laughed.

Doris looked like she needed and wanted to hear more.

Tyler searched his memory for something more he could share with her. "Your son can be quite spontaneous. Did he tell you about our polka at the country club?"

Doris shot a look at her son, "Oh, my. Now where was I when that happened?"

"On your Mediterranean cruise, Mother," Christopher replied.

Doris was delighted. "I'll bet that turned a few heads."

"One or two is all." Christopher provided her with an answer.

Maria came in and announced that lunch was ready.

"This way," Doris said rising.

Christopher took his mother's arm, and Tyler followed. Doris leaned over to Christopher and whispered, "I think that I like him."

Tyler smiled and took another sip of his martini. During lunch, Doris said she wasn't planning on going to Palm Springs until after the holidays and asked what Christopher's and Tyler's plans were? Christopher thought that he would like to host Christmas this year.

They would have dinner on Christmas Day. Since Christopher was telling his mother about what a great cook Tyler was, Tyler offered to prepare the Christmas dinner. "I only ask that you tell me what you like. It can be a time for us to start a new tradition, Christmas together. I want you to enjoy it."

Doris and Christopher said in unison, "Prime rib."

Piece of cake, thought Tyler. Silently, Tyler expressed his gratitude that meeting Christopher's mother was going so smoothly. Excited, Tyler couldn't wait. "It's going to be the best Christmas ever!"

CHAPTER TWENTY FOUR

Two weeks before Christmas, Christopher and Tyler searched for the perfect Christmas tree for Christopher's house. Tyler put his tree up the day after Thanksgiving. Since his went up so early, he always had an artificial tree that was as real looking as one could ask for. Christopher insisted on a live tree, so he could smell the fresh pine. After a lot of looking, they found an eight-foot Douglas Fir. It would look majestic in the great room under the beamed ceiling. At the tree farm where they found it, the owners put the tree on some powerful vibrating machine that shook any and all dried needles out of it. They then bore a hole in the base of the trunk so the tree could anchor onto the spike in the tree stand. Once bundled in twine for transport, the tree easily slid into the back of Christopher's SUV. *How many vehicles did he have anyway?* Tyler sometimes wondered. He seemed to have one for every occasion. The red Ford Expedition was the perfect vehicle for today.

Once home, with the tree standing in what was to be its location through New Year's Eve, Tyler fixed sandwiches for lunch while the tree warmed up. "A tree that large is going to require lots of lights. Do you have enough?" he asked Christopher.

"I think so. If not, we'll get more."

After lunch, Tyler helped Christopher carry boxes of lights and decorations up from the storage area in the lower level. The ornaments were obviously from years past, but the lights were new.

"I bought all miniature blue LED lights. I thought it would be pretty. What do you think?" Christopher asked, seeking Tyler's approval. "I didn't want to copy yours, which is all white lights, which is beautiful, but I didn't want the same thing."

"It will be gorgeous."

They began putting on the strings of lights, carefully weaving them in and out of the branches. Christopher got on the step ladder and started at the top. Tyler assisted him as needed after the process began. Tyler thought that this was the most tedious part of putting up a tree. When they finished, they turned on the lights, and the thousand-plus blue lights were a beautiful sight to behold.

"Awesome!"

Tyler opened another large bag and to his surprise found it full of white bubble lights. "Bubble lights! I love bubble lights! How did we overlook these? Please add them. Your tree will be magnificent then."

Christopher soon added them to the tree. It reminded him of the sky lit up on a clear night. It was an impressively-lit tree. The two men quickly hung the ornaments. Many of them Christopher had obtained from his mother and had been in his family for years. There were even a couple of ornaments that he had made as a child in school for his parents. Each one had a memory behind it. Tyler loved listening to Christopher tell about each ornament as they decorated the tree.

"I brought an ornament for the top, Christopher." Tyler opened a box which he had brought along. It contained a large male angel attired in dark red cloth carrying a lantern. The angel looked majestic sitting at the tree's top. "He's smiling down on us, Christopher," his arm around Christopher's waist as they stood back and admired their day's work.

Next they set the poinsettias that Tyler had brought from the shop around the room. There were twelve, six red and six white. "Why did you bring a dozen?" Christopher wanted to know.

"They represent the Twelve Days of Christmas."

Tyler put another couple of pieces of wood on the fire. Sadie was curled up by the fireplace. Christopher had made hot cocoa to drink. The two men sat next to each other on the sofa, gazing into the fire. That and the Christmas tree provided the perfect ambience for the room. Christopher leaned over and kissed Tyler on the forehead. "I am so blessed, Tyler. We are so lucky to have each other and all of this."

"I know. Thank you for being the man you are and for wanting me in your life."

Sadie, awakened from her nap, came over to the two men and put her nose between the space where their legs were touching each other. "Sadie thanks you, too." With that, Sadie jumped up onto the sofa and sat directly on Christopher's lap.

"Well, this is a first," Christopher said smiling.

"It's unanimous. We both love you."

The winter months were brutal. There was heavy snowfall often accompanied by wind chill temperatures below zero. However, Christopher and Tyler didn't let that affect their outlook in the least. They were at one or the other's house every weekend. When anyone complained about the cold and abundance of snow, either man's stock answer was, "It's a Michigan winter. Get over it."

On the clear, crisp days, they would go sledding or tobogganing. Tyler loved being on the toboggan with Christopher tightly behind him, each hanging on firmly to the other. "Here we go, Sport!"

Christopher would say as they began the descent down the steep hill. What a rush! "More fun than a roller coaster," Tyler replied.

Tyler and Christopher hadn't had a discussion about money and who was paying for what for some time. Tyler paid for things when he could but knew that he couldn't ever keep up with Christopher because his income was nowhere near his. He resigned himself to this. However, if they were really going to get married, although a date hadn't been set, Tyler was determined that Christopher be very well aware in black and white that should things fall apart after the wedding, that he wasn't going to seek financial remuneration. That was another reason Tyler didn't want to sell his house. He wanted a place to call home, should he need to. Deep down, he harbored a fear that this idyllic relationship wouldn't last forever. So, Tyler drafted a simple document stating that should his forthcoming marriage to Christopher Matthew Girrardi be terminated for any reason, he would not seek any of Christopher's assets. Tyler would take with him what he brought to the marriage. He signed and dated it and placed it in an envelope with Christopher's name on it. He would hand it to Christopher the next time he was over. There. He did it.

When Christopher got over to Tyler's that night, Tyler handed Christopher the envelope.

"What's this?"

"I wrote and signed a prenuptial agreement stating that if our marriage ends, I don't want any of your money or things, just what I brought to the marriage."

"Gee, that's a really good sign that you expect us to stay together."

"I do, Christopher. But I also want you to know that it's not about your wealth. It never has been. I know I've told you, but now it's in writing. It's not written in 'fancy legalese.' I have to do this."

"Okay, I will look at it. I suppose I need to give you one stating the same for me."

"If you want to. I'm not asking you to."

"Okay, Tyler, we'll discuss this later. There is something else I really need to run by you. Can we go in the living room and sit?"

"Yes. What is it?"

"You're pretty intuitive. How are you at figuring out dreams and what they mean?"

"I can tell you what I think it means, but ultimately, you have to figure out what it symbolizes to you. So, tell me."

Christopher went into great detail about his recurring dream that he had been having. "I'm walking down this very white, wide sidewalk. It appears to be made of alabaster. On each side of the walk are various fruit trees. There are apple trees, orange trees, peach trees, cherry trees. I mean there is an apple tree, next to a peach tree, next to an orange tree, etc. They aren't in groves. All of these trees are next to each other, lining the sidewalk. Each tree is loaded with ripe fruit. The branches are bending down toward the green grass beneath. They are so loaded with fruit that the branches can hardly support the weight. As I'm walking down the walk-way looking at all of these trees, I see several men all wearing white robes seated at a long white table. I'm wearing a white robe too. It has a hood on it, but the hood is not on my head. It is laying down on my shoulders and back. I'm approaching this table of men. I feel that they are old, wise, and well-respected. They have something to tell me. I feel each of them has a message for me. I feel they are evaluating me for my job or something I've done. I approach the table slowly. The man on the end motions for me to step closer. I get scared and freeze. I'm afraid to go closer. I'm afraid to hear what he and the others might say to me. As he rises, he removes the hood from his head and smiles at me, but I'm too scared to talk. Then I wake up. What do you think that means?"

"You said that you are wearing a white robe like theirs?"

"Yes."

"Perhaps you are in training to become one of them. Like an apprentice. To me, the fruit trees represent abundance. They are ready to be harvested. The fact that there are a variety of fruit trees means that your abundance is not all coming from the same source. However, abundance on several levels, several avenues, are yours for the picking. White is a very spiritual color. Your white robe means this is about your spiritual path."

"Okay."

"These men or beings may be guides or ascended masters or members of the Great White Brotherhood."

"What's that? The Great White Brotherhood?"

"It is also known as the Brotherhood of Light. It is made up of Cosmic Beings, Angels, and Ascended Masters. Much has been written about it. I have a couple of books about it which I can loan to you or you can, of course, Google it."

Tyler explained what he knew of the Great White Brotherhood. It is a spiritual organization composed of those Ascended Masters who have arisen from our Earth into immortality. It has been written that those Masters said that they would not leave their brothers and sisters on Earth behind. They would stay and assist. The energies are such now that the door is open; the veil is being lifted. Some of the more well-known members of this Brotherhood and Sisterhood includes Jesus the Christ, Gautama Buddha, Mother Teresa, and many other Ascended Teachers of mankind. It would also include members of the Heavenly Host, such as Archangel Michael and the Spiritual Hierarchy directly concerned with the Spiritual Progress of our world. The word "white" does not refer to race, but rather to the aura or halo of the White Light of the Christ that surrounds the saints and sages of all ages and come from all nations.

"I reiterate, it's not a race issue. It's not a bunch of white guys dressed in white talking to other white guys. Did you see his face, the man who beckoned you to come closer?"

"A little. I think he had a darker complexion. His dark eyes sparkled with warmth. That is all I remember. I woke up."

"What do you think it means? Look at each part. What do those fruits symbolize to you? The men sitting at the table, and so on."

"I don't know what to think."

Tyler shared the advice he knew would work. "Tonight, just before you go to sleep, ask to have a clarifying dream so that you can clearly understand what the message is here for you. Ask to be shown in a loving way what this panel of apparently wise men have to say to you."

"Why was I afraid to move closer?"

"I don't know. If you're afraid, ask them if they are from the Light. I'm pretty sure that they are. Remember, the Light will always triumph over Darkness."

"Okay, thanks."

"I think it's a good dream." Tyler paused to listen to what his Guides were telling him. "I'm hearing that much will be revealed to you in the Dream State. Blessings Be."

CHAPTER TWENTY FIVE

Saint Patrick's Day called for a corned beef and cabbage. Tyler had invited old friends Dennis and Michael as well as George and Al to dinner and to meet Christopher. All of this time had passed and he hadn't introduced them.

"It's about time, Blanche." Dennis seldom called any of his close male friends by their given name.

Michael and Dennis were in their 40's, single, and liked it that way. George and Al, both in their early 50's had been together for ten years and ran a highly successful antique store. They also conducted estate sales and auctions and had an excellent reputation for knowing their product and what their customers wanted.

"I'm looking forward to meeting your friends at last," Christopher said as he was setting the wine glasses on the table.

"Me, too. They'll adore you."

Dinner went well as all the men loved good conversation accompanied by good food. Topics ranged from what was happening locally, to travel, film, theater, and more.

"We'll have you over to my place for dinner in May after Tyler moves in."

Dennis spoke for all of them. "Tyler, why aren't you already living with your handsome beau? I would be if I were in your shoes."

"I'm waiting until Spring to move in. That's what we decided."

"Okay," but George reminded him, "technically Spring begins in three days on the 20th. No need to wait until May."

"Thank you all, but I'll let you know if I move sooner."

That weekend, Christopher and Tyler travelled to Chicago for the weekend. While there, they attended a rock and gem show. The event featured a minimum of one hundred vendors selling every size and shape of every geode imaginable. Other vendors featured a variety of jewelry. Earrings, matching necklaces, rings, all were waiting for the correct buyer.

As they were strolling around, Christopher walked over to a table and picked up a piece of citrine the size of small dinner plate that had the upper left portion broken off. The amber colored stone rested on a dark wooden base. "Look at this, Tyler."

"It's gorgeous."

Tyler picked up a book on gem stones the dealer had on the table for his buyers to reference. The keywords for citrine were success, abundance, and personal power.

"Look at this. This stone is you!"

"No wonder I like it," Christopher replied placing the rock back on its stand.

The next vendor had only amethyst displayed. Every size and shape imaginable, including some that were cut into heart-shaped stones which would easily fill the entire palm of one's hand, were available for purchase. "Oh, my," Tyler gasped. In the center stood the largest amethyst geode he had ever seen. It was at least four-and-a-half feet tall and eighteen inches wide at the base. The points of its many facets were the darkest purple. Towards the top center there was a clear quartz crystal highlighting the surrounding dark violet. The price tag was $10,000.

"That would look great with the rest of your collection." "Yes, it would. But, no, you're not going to get that for me. That's too much."

They finished looking at the exhibit and were ready to leave. "I'll be right back, Christopher. I need to visit the restroom before we head back to the hotel."

Christopher waited by the exit. Tyler half ran to the citrine vendor's table. If the piece that Christopher looked at was still there, he was going to buy it for him. It was. What luck!

Christopher was waiting patiently at the door. "What did you buy on your way to pee?"

"I'll show you in the car." They walked to the parking lot and quickly got in the car. "I was going to wait until we got back to the hotel, but I want you to open this now."

Christopher carefully opened the large bag and removed the plastic bubble wrap revealing the gorgeous piece of citrine he had admired earlier in the afternoon. "What? Tyler, it's beautiful. Thank you," as he kissed him.

"I thought it would look great on your desk. It's you."

Tyler smiled. It was another moment of many he shared with his love that weekend.

It was the end of March when Doris Girrardi returned from Palm Springs. She called Tyler at work and asked if he would meet her for lunch. Could they have lunch, just the two of them, without Christopher knowing?

Even though Tyler was busy, he did block out time to have lunch with Christopher's mother. Although he wasn't thrilled about keeping it a secret, he did as his mother requested. Tyler met her at Patty's. Doris was already seated and had ordered a half carafe of white wine and was already sipping on it. She looked very smart in her navy blue suit, very business-like.

"Mrs. Girrardi, all tan and radiant!"

Doris hugged Tyler, "It's good to see you. Do sit. I hope you don't mind, but I took the liberty of ordering some wine. I do hope it's to your liking."

"That's fine, Mrs. Girrardi. I hope you haven't been waiting long." Doris started to fill Tyler's glass. "Half a glass for me is plenty. I have to go back to work after lunch." Tyler needed to keep his wits about him as well.

After small talk, Doris Girrardi went right to the heart of why she wanted to lunch with Tyler without Christopher present.

"Tyler, Christopher is all the family I have. He's a fine man."

"I couldn't agree with you more."

"How serious are you about Chris? I know I have no control over matters of the heart, but I do not want to see him get hurt. Not again. Do you love him? I mean really, truly love him?"

"Yes, with all my heart. Mrs. Girrardi—"

"Call me Dori. All my friends do. I would like for us to be friends, Tyler."

Smiling, Tyler went on, "Dori, Christopher is my knight-in-shining-armour. I didn't encourage him at all when we first met. He was married to Karen then, and I was just getting over a relationship that went sour. Someone whom I loved very much who one day decided he didn't want me anymore."

"You've experienced pain, too. It does give us compassion, doesn't it? Have you always been gay?"

"Yes. My sexual orientation is the one thing that I have always been certain of."

Doris elaborated on how she thought Christopher had always been attracted to men, although she never said anything to anyone. However, there are some things that a "mother just knows in her heart."

Tyler told Doris that he had never known such kindness, or respect, or ever known a loving, masculine man who wasn't afraid to stand up for what he knew in his heart was right. "For the longest time, I resisted him, thinking perhaps I was just a guinea pig for him, so he could figure things out for himself. I didn't want to be that. Been there, done that. But because of his persistence, and love, I luckily realized that Christopher was being one-hundred-percent sincere. He is the real deal. That is so hard to find."

"My son is a kind, generous man."

"You said that you didn't want to see Christopher hurt again. Are you referring to the demise of his marriage? I had nothing to do with that."

"Oh, honey, I know you didn't. Karen was just a gold-digging slut. I never liked her much. I'll tell you why. She only cared enough about Chris to get some money and live the high-life. She never made him happy. I honestly don't know what they had in common. He married her for all of the wrong reasons. I told him the morning of the wedding day that he didn't have to go through with it. He insisted. Did you ever meet her?"

"She came in the shop once with Christopher when they were still together. I didn't know them then. To speak frankly, I didn't like her attitude. They left. I never gave her another thought."

Doris was silent and deep in thought as she sipped her wine.

Doris went on, "I have NEVER seen Christopher as happy as he is now, with you. I don't want his heart to get broken."

"Why do you think I would?"

"Did Christopher ever tell you about his fraternity brother, Alec, from his college days?"

"No." *He did tell me about Alec Stanton. Did I just lie to my future mother-in-law?*

Doris Girrardi was finally able to talk to someone about this topic that had bothered her for years. She went into detail about Alec Stanton, Christopher's handsome, congenial friend from high school and college. They were best buddies, played football together in high school, and joined the same fraternity at Purdue University. Alec always had girls after him. So did Chris but he never seemed very interested, but Alec encouraged it. Chris never dated much in high school or college, which was when she started to surmise that maybe her son was gay. "I know that he loved Alec."

"Like a brother?"

"I think that Chris wanted more and when he told Alec how he felt, Alec rejected him. He told him that he never wanted to see him again because he wasn't 'like that.'"

"And Christopher told you this?'

"No, not in so many words. When I questioned him about Alec's sudden disappearance from his life, Christopher said they had parted as friends, it wasn't pleasant and he didn't want to discuss it." However, Doris insisted she knew that the ending of that relationship broke Christopher's heart. Alec had gotten married a couple of years later. Christopher wasn't invited, nor was Doris, which she thought odd since she had known his parents as well.

"Christopher always tells me what a great relationship he has with you and had with his father and how he could always tell you anything."

"That's true. He always told us everything. Everything except the details concerning the end of his friendship with Alec."

Suddenly, Tyler recalled the first words Christopher had ever spoken to him. "You can't help who you fall in love with, can you?"

"All I'm really trying to say here today, Tyler, is that I like you. You make my son happy. That's all I have ever wanted for him. I want him to have someone who loves him as much as Chris loves that person in return. I want him to have a partner to share his life with and to grow old together with."

"I wish you were my mother."

"I kind of will be once you two get married. However, you can't do that here in this backward state. Not yet, anyway. Fucking Fundamentalist Republicans!"

"Dori, I think I love you more already!"

"Have you two set a date yet?"

"No, we haven't talked about it a lot. I told Christopher I want to live with him for awhile first, just to be sure we don't make each other too crazy."

"You're a wise man. If Chris had lived with Karen first, I don't think that they would have married. Oh well, that's water under the bridge. Let's order."

"You must come to see my shop after lunch. Let me send some flowers home with you for your table. Please."

"Okay, I will. Another nice thing that I noticed is that my son doesn't seem to mind that you always address him as Christopher. He hasn't let anyone else do that since he was a little boy. It's nice to hear. I like it." Raising her wine glass, "First, I want to offer a toast: to you and me, Tyler, and our new friendship."

Tyler raised his glass and let it clink with Dori's. He drank the chilled sweet moscato wine. He knew that he would never ask Christopher about Alec Stanton. He didn't need to.

CHAPTER TWENTY SIX

Christopher had asked Tyler to make his favorite meal, scalloped potatoes and "pizza meatloaf." It would be the last meal they shared together in Tyler's house. Tyler was all set to move in with Christopher the following week and had started to pack things in boxes for the move. Once moved, he would rent his house to Sophie.

Tyler mused as he mixed the beaten egg and spaghetti sauce and added the parmesan cheese and oregano together. He stirred in the old-fashioned oatmeal--quick oats would not do--extra chopped onion, and mushrooms. Then, he mixed in the extra lean ground round beef with his hands. Next, he spread the mixture out on a large piece of waxed paper and molded the meat into a rectangular shape. Shredded mozzarella cheese was sprinkled on top of the meat; then he placed the turkey pepperoni on top of that before rolling it as if it were a big jelly roll. Once the rolled loaf was placed in the baking pan, he spread the remaining spaghetti sauce on top of the meatloaf. It gave Tyler great pleasure to prepare meals for Christopher. He was always so appreciative of his efforts in the kitchen. In fact, Christopher seldom let a time, a date, an event shared with Tyler go by without commenting on the quality time they had just spent together. *Tyler, you are one lucky man to have Christopher in your life,* as he smilingly put the meatloaf in the oven next to the scalloped potatoes which were starting to bubble.

Scalloped potatoes. He would never forget the first time he made them for Christopher.

"Where did you get these potatoes? They're excellent! What brand are they?"

"I don't know. Idaho I guess."

"No, what brand? Don't they come in a box and you just add milk? I don't know. I'm not the cook you are. The few times I made these, they tasted like cardboard."

"I peeled and sliced real potatoes and peeled and chopped the onions myself. I made the cream sauce from butter, flour, and milk and then poured it over the potatoes."

"You made these from scratch?"

"Yeah, that's how I cook."

"That takes a lot of time."

"Yes, more time than that instant shit in a box with who knows what kind of preservatives added to it. But much better tasting and better for you."

"I'm impressed."

Tyler couldn't help but think, *I just won this man's heart with scalloped potatoes. Imagine that.*

"I had some help. I mean, I didn't grow the potatoes or onions in my garden, nor did I milk the cow or churn the butter. I had help in that respect."

Christopher smiled, "Smart ass." Then raising his wine glass to Tyler, "To your culinary skills."

Tyler raised his glass in kind, "To the chef's guest."

Tyler glanced at the clock and realized that Christopher would be here soon. He hurriedly set the table, holding up the wine glasses making sure that there weren't any water spots on them. He loved these evenings with Christopher. Life was good. This thought dominated his mind as he went about setting the table, which always included candles and fresh flowers.

The two men made small talk during dinner, not even consciously aware that the silent moments were often punctuated with smiling eyes directed at the other. Perhaps to a silent observer, the two men would appear "too much in love with each other, infatuated, or sickeningly sweet." So what? The two men only had eyes for each other. They talked of having a huge party in the early summer. They would both invite people they knew. It was time that they expanded their circle of mutual friends.

Following dinner, Tyler offered, "Would you like some coffee and/or a cordial to go with dessert?"

"This was excellent. What's for dessert?"

"Chocolate raspberry cake."

"Just coffee for now. Maybe some cake a little later."

"Coming right up."

Christopher helped Tyler clear the table. While in the kitchen waiting for the coffee to finish brewing, Christopher asked, "Tyler, I know I said that we could live together 'in sin' as you say, but have you given any thought to our wedding? What kind of ceremony do you want and where?"

"What do you want?"

"Oh, no you don't. I asked you first. You tell me."

"I want something simple. We still can't get legally married in this state, so we need to go somewhere where we can. But I want something simple with just you and me and your mother present. Sophie was recently ordained as a Coptic minister. I know that she'd perform the ceremony."

"I'd like that. I'm ignorant here. What exactly is a Coptic minister?"

Tyler explained. The Coptics were originally known as the Essenes. Joseph and Mary were Essenes and when they took Jesus and fled from Harrod, they went into the land that is now known as Egypt. It was the Essenes who hid them and helped raise Jesus. It was the Essenes who helped Jesus learn how to be the Mystic and Master he would become while on Earth. The Essenes later became known as the Coptics.

"If I was going to go to a church, it would be a Coptic church. Would you be okay with that?"

"Yes, what else?"

"I would like to get married on the beach just before sunset. I want us to each wear a white shirt that has a pattern in it. White on white, maybe linen, and some nice jeans. We could wear sandals but barefoot is good, too. I'd want *Pachelbel's Canon in D* played on violins at the beginning. Of course, I want us to write our own vows. What do you want?"

"That sounds really good to me. I had a big church wedding before, lots of attendants and all that went with it. It became such a big circus. I hated it. So what you propose sounds good to me. We can work together on the ceremony."

"Of course."

"Maybe when we get back from our honeymoon, we can have a reception at the house for our friends, something easy—appetizers, cocktails, and music."

"Sure, but no gifts. We could put it on the invitations that in lieu of gifts, bring some non-perishable food items that will be donated to a food pantry or gifts of money will be given to the Heifer Project or something like that. We don't really need anything."

"Agreed. Any ideas where you want to go for our honeymoon? I am going to spoil you on this trip, so don't tell me something simple like a weekend in Chicago."

Tyler thought a moment. "Italy. I want to spend time in Tuscany. Then to Venice and to ride in a gondola. Let's go see the Sistine Chapel and the Colosseum. Where do you want to go, Christopher?"

"I want to travel the world with you. We go to Italy for our honeymoon; but then I choose the destination of our next trip."

"That's a deal, handsome." They kissed but were interrupted by the very loud crack of thunder.

"That doesn't sound good. I didn't know we were supposed to have a storm."

Tyler turned on the TV, and together they saw that a severe thunderstorm warning was in effect with high winds and hail. There was also the strong possibility that a funnel cloud would form.

Christopher said, "Babe, wrap up some of that dessert, and I'll take it with me. I want to get home before that storm hits."

"I don't want you out there on the road in this weather. What's so important that you have to get home right now?"

"I have something to take care of. I need to make sure it's okay."

"What?"

"It's a surprise. Please don't ask me anymore about it."

"But—"

"But nothing. Trust me. I need to leave and take care of it before the storm hits."

Tyler wrapped up two large pieces of chocolate raspberry cake. "Promise me you'll call the second you get home."

"I always do."

They kissed quickly, "I love you, Christopher."

"I love you, too. I think I'm the luckiest guy alive. You're the best!"

With that, Christopher sped out of the driveway heading for his house.

Tyler went back inside his house. "Sadie, I don't feel good about this storm."

He went to his altar, lit the candles, and looking upward, invoked the Angels: "Archangels Michael, Raphael, Gabrielle, and Uriel, please protect Christopher, and get him home safely. Thank you. And so it is."

Outside, the dark clouds picked up their speed, and rain started to pummel the earth as Tyler and Sadie silently waited for Christopher's phone call.

CHAPTER TWENTY SEVEN

It was 9:00 p.m. when Christopher left Tyler's. He should have easily been back home in thirty to forty-five minutes at the latest. The monsoon-like rain continued incessantly. At the storm's onset, Tyler and Sadie settled in on the sofa. Every few minutes Tyler prayed, "Please Creator, keep Christopher safe." At 10:15 Tyler called Christopher on his cell phone, but it went right to voice mail. Five minutes later, he sent Christopher a text. "I thought you'd have gotten home by now. Please let me know when you get there. Love you. T."

10:30 came and went by. Tyler started pacing. He went to the window, pulled the curtains back, and watched the rain angrily hit the pane. The clock chimed 11:00. Still no word from Christopher. "Sadie, what do you think is going on with Christopher? Maybe his phone died. Still he could have called me from his land line. I guess the storm took that out, too. Sadie, let's camp out here on the sofa tonight." He closed his eyes and prayed earnestly. Sadie whimpered as the clock struck twelve.

He lit more candles that were on the coffee table. Against one wall the table lamp was on the lowest level of a three-way bulb. The sound of the driving rain continued to hammer against the windows. At 1:30 a.m., Tyler was jolted to the present moment by the doorbell ringing and a loud knocking on the front door. Barking, Sadie beat him to the door and stood guard. Tyler pulled the curtain aside just enough to see that there was a state police car parked in his driveway.

Opening the door he saw two officers standing there. "Yes, officers?"

"Tyler Reynolds?"

"Yes, that's me."

"Do you know a Christopher Girrardi?"

"Yes. Is he alright? What's happened?"

"He was in a bad accident. Inside his wallet, there was an index card folded with your name and address and a note saying that if anything ever happened to him to contact you."

"Where is he? How badly is he hurt?"

The second officer, silent to this point asked, "Are you his next of kin?"

"Christopher is my fiancé. Please tell me what's happened."

"Mr. Girrardi was in a very bad accident on Cline Road, not far from his residence. An oncoming car, swerved over the center line into Mr. Girrardi's lane. In an effort to avoid impact, his car spun out of control, rolling over several times." The officer paused. "There were no survivors."

Tyler could not begin to comprehend what the officer had just stated. "What are you saying? Are you saying," his voice trailed off, "that Christopher is dead?"

"Yes, sir."

Tyler thought that his knees were going to buckle out from under him. Reaching out to grab the first officer for support, "My

Christopher?! No." Fighting back tears, "No, it can't be. Are you sure? Are you certain it was Christopher Girrardi of 4849 Mulberry Lane?"

"Yes, sir."

The first officer noticing the color draining from Tyler's face, "Take a breath, sir. Breathe."

"Yeah."

"Does Mr. Girrardi have any living blood relatives we should contact?"

Dazed, Tyler mumbled, "Yes. His mother, Doris Girrardi. I'll get you her phone number and address." Retrieving the information and giving it to the officer, Tyler went on. "Please, let me go with you to tell her. It's not right for me to know and not be there when you tell her."

"We can do that. Do you have a good relationship with her?"

"I certainly do."

The second officer went on, "If she is currently the next of kin, she will have to go to the morgue to identify the body."

"Of course. Would one of you mind driving my car to Doris' house. I would appreciate it."

The two officers looked at each other. "Okay. Drive his car Mike. You follow me."

"Thank you."

Extinguishing the candles, Tyler grabbed his wallet and his jacket. He gave the address of Doris' residence to both officers. He would call Sophie later and have her check in on Sadie before she went to Tyler's Floral and Gifts to begin the day's work.

Tyler and the officers began the drive to Doris Girrardi's home. They rode in silence. *Keep it together, Tyler.* But he couldn't stop crying. He dabbed his eyes with his handkerchief. *This is a fucking nightmare. I wish that I could wake up and know that it isn't really happening.*

He thought he should call Dori when they got to her driveway to wake her up. He mentioned this to Officer Mike whose response was, "Please let us take care of it." *Okay, I won't argue.* His mind raced as he drove along. *Christopher, why didn't you stay at my house as I asked you to do? If I had moved in with Christopher earlier, this would never have happened. Christopher would have already been home. But no, I wanted to wait until spring to move. That was a stupid decision, wasn't it?*

When Tyler and the officers arrived at Dori's house, they walked up to the front door and rang the bell. Maria, the housekeeper answered the door. The officers needed to speak to Doris right away. "I'll wake her," said Maria as she ascended the stairway. Lights went on upstairs in the huge house. Minutes later, Doris Girrardi, flanked by her housekeeper, came hurriedly down the stairs. Taking one look at Tyler and the police, Doris knew. "It's Christopher, isn't it?"

The police quickly told Doris Girrardi the same story they told Tyler previously. They concluded it with explaining why Tyler was with them. Throughout hearing the news of her son's death, Doris remained stoic. When some of the shock wore off, she let her guard down. Clutching Maria, a long slow wail originating in her toes rose all the way up through her person. Maria, crying as well, held her employer and friend.

The officer in charge said, "I'm so sorry, Mrs. Girrardi." Eventually her anguish subsided. After the police left, Maria and Tyler on either side of Doris sat on the sofa saying nothing.

Taking a deep breath, "I can't do this alone, Tyler. Please help me."

"You know I will."

"We have to identify the body. Go with me. Then we need to make arrangements for his funeral."

Tyler thought a moment and said, "Yes, of course. When do you think we should go to the hospital's morgue?"

"In the morning. What time is it now?"

Maria answered. "It's 4:30."

"I'll be ready by 9:00 a.m. sharp."

"Try to get some rest, Dori."

"You too, Tyler. You go lie down in the guest room. Maria, please show him."

Saying nothing, Doris and Tyler hugged each other and headed upstairs to their respective rooms with Maria closely behind them.

Once in the room that he and Christopher had shared here, Tyler kicked off his shoes. He saw the white pillar candle on the dresser that they had used the last time they had shared this room. Tyler instinctively went over and lit the candle. Looking upward, "Why didn't you protect Christopher and keep him safe? I don't understand." Tyler paused and stared at the flame. "I ask now that Christopher already be in the Light. My petition is that he went directly into the Light. Thank you."

He walked over to the bed and lay down. Turning on his side, he clutched the pillow closely to his abdomen and sobbed quietly until he was overcome by sleep.

"TYLER!" Tyler bolted upright in the bed. He had distinctly heard Christopher call out his name. Suddenly the grim reality returned.

Neither Dori or Tyler slept much. Tyler stopped at a Starbucks and got two coffees. They proceeded to the morgue. Neither of them had much to say as they drove to the hospital. "Lots of sticks and small branches down from the storm last night," Tyler commented.

"Yes, there are." They drove along in silence. It required less energy. Both Doris and Tyler were inherently aware of how much energy each would need to get through this experience.

When they got to the hospital, the receptionist directed them to the morgue. The corridors were silent, cold, and the floors faintly smelled of the cleanser used to mop them. Following the signage, they found the morgue and told the attending medical examiner why they were there.

"This way," he said.

"Could you tell us if—," Dori's voice faltered. "Do you know if death was instant, or did he suffer?"

In his head Tyler pleaded, *Please tell us it was instant, that he didn't suffer an iota.*

"At the rate of speed the other driver was going when he hit your son's vehicle, I'd say his death was instantaneous."

"Thank you, God." Tyler muttered.

"Please be aware there are some cuts and bruises on his face. His air bag did not release for some reason. Even if it had, I doubt it would have saved him."

Tyler and Dori followed the medical examiner into the lab. There were two bodies on tables with sheets covering them. Tyler presumed that the body on the other table belonged to the driver that had hit Christopher. The examiner pulled back the sheet to reveal Christopher's ashen colored, bruised face. Tyler choked back a sob. Dori gasped and squeezed his hand so hard that under other circumstances he would have said something, but the fact was that the squeezing of each other's hands is what helped them keep it together.

"That's my son. That's Christopher."

"Yes," was all Tyler could whisper.

"That is what death looks like, Tyler."

"Uh, huh." It was all Tyler could do to not let out an anguished scream. *I will do that privately,* he told himself. *Be strong, now.*

The examiner covered Christopher's face back up, and they walked silently out of the room together. "Do you have a funeral director that you would like us to contact? We will need you to sign a release form."

Tyler looked at Doris and said, "Could you give us a moment?"

"Certainly."

They walked over to a pair of chairs by a table and sat. "Tyler, we need to discuss things." She paused, "I'm in favor of cremation."

"We can't leave him looking like this. First, I want him to be cleaned up and dressed in his finest suit. I think his navy blue one with a white shirt and red tie. I want to--I NEED to see him that way first. We just can't leave him like this. Then the cremation can take place. Please."

"I want that too. We'll have a viewing. His body will be there for the funeral service. Then the cremation can occur. I'd like his ashes buried in our family plot."

"That's fine."

"So much to think about and to plan. Oh, God." Doris stared silently at her folded hands.

"I don't know about a minister. I never really had an affinity for organized religion. Last I knew, Christopher didn't have one either. I know that when he was married, he and Karen went to that Church of the Open Door a couple of times."

"He really wasn't into organized religion. I have a friend who is a Coptic minister. I can ask Sophie. She knew Christopher."

Doris decided on a funeral home to handle the arrangements and Tyler contacted the director for her.

"Thanks." Fortified by a sudden burst of adrenalin and resolve, "Let's forge ahead and get this done. Do you have a key to Chris's house? Let's stop and get his clothes to bury him in. When we meet with the funeral director later today, we can take them with us."

When they got to Christopher's house and went inside, Tyler keyed in the security code. They walked through the strangely silent house.

Why does it seem so weird, so eerie to be here? Tyler wondered.

They went upstairs to Christopher's room. The bed was neatly made; everything in its place. Tyler led the way to the huge walk-in closet. He noticed all of the clothes from one side had been removed. Christopher had told him he had moved a lot of his clothing so there would be room for Tyler's clothing along with Christopher's.

"Why is this side empty?" Doris asked.

"That's where I was to hang my clothes when I moved in next week."

Tyler quickly found the suit he had in mind. "What do you think, Dori? Is this suit okay along with a white shirt and a tie with lots of red in it? Red is a power color, you know. Christopher told me that he always wore a tie with red when he met with the Board or with an important client."

Dori found a red tie that she had given to Christopher. Tyler found a white dress shirt. It was then that Tyler saw the casual white linen shirt with the subtle white flower pattern in it hanging with the tags still on it. "This must have been the shirt that he said he already bought for our wedding. How did he know it's what I would have chosen?" Tyler said half-aloud. "Dori, I would like to take this shirt if I may. It's the one that Christopher said he would wear when we exchanged our vows."

"Sure."

Tyler then quickly went to the dresser and pulled out clean underwear and socks and picked up a pair of Christopher's black leather dress shoes. "I think we have everything now."

On the nightstand next to the bed was a yellow legal pad. In Christopher's hand writing at the top, it read: Things to do before Tyler moves in. Christopher had listed items: clean out closet, order fresh roses, prepare meditation room. All of the items were checked off except the one about the roses. *Was this what you had to get back to work on, Christopher? What was so important that you braved the storm for?*

It was almost noon as they stopped on the way back to Dori's house and had breakfast, though neither was very hungry. "We need to eat something, Tyler, to keep up our strength. The next few days are going to be rough."

Back at Dori's, they had time for a short nap before heading to the funeral home to make arrangements. Tyler stretched out on the bed in the guest room and slept hard for an hour.

Again he heard, "TYLER!" He awoke with a start, knowing Christopher had called out his name. Was it all a bad dream? No, sadly it wasn't.

CHAPTER TWENTY EIGHT

The next day at work, Tyler realized again how lucky he was to have Sophie in his life. Not only was she a great friend, but she naturally assumed the running of Tyler's Floral and Gifts. Things were going as smoothly as if Tyler was in charge. Sophie and Tyler were often on the same page about things, so it was no surprise to him that she did what he would have done if the roles were reversed. Sophie knew Tyler would be no help in running the shop this week. She went ahead and hired a part time girl. Kara had come in about two weeks ago looking for work. She knew enough about the flower business to be an asset and she followed instructions to the letter. Sophie knew she had made a good choice hiring Kara. She started immediately. If need be, there would be no problem increasing her hours.

All Tyler wanted at the moment was to focus on the two arrangements that he was making for Christopher's funeral. He went into the walk-in cooler and stared blankly at his current inventory. *Where to start?* Dori wanted roses, lots of them, from her. Tyler thought that yellow ones would look rich against the cherry casket.

He was still undecided as to what the arrangement from him would be. *Make the arrangement from Dori first. That will give you a little more time to decide, Tyler.* He went to work and an hour later was putting the finishing touches on the blanket of roses that would grace the casket. He put it in the cooler for the time being. He sat on the stool at the work station and stared at the empty vase in front of him.

"How are you doing?" Sophie asked as she checked in on him.

"I don't know where to start on his flowers. I SHOULD know."

"What were his favorite flowers? His favorite colors?" Sophie handed him a blank legal pad and a pen. "Brainstorm. Make a list. That will help."

"It has to be magnificent."

"It will be."

Picking up the pen, Tyler started listing: red roses, stargazer lilies, salmon or pink roses, sunflowers, purple liatris, yellow snapdragons, and red gerberas? He wanted something with lots of color, something that said joy and love. Whatever he decided on creating, it just HAD to be magnificent.

Sophie told him not to worry so much about his arrangement. "I'm sure Christopher will like it because you made it. Tyler, nodding in agreement, couldn't help but blink back tears.

"Are you sure you don't mind conducting his funeral? You're the only one I trust. Dori is fine with that. I'm so fortunate that she has been so great towards me. You know others in my situation would be shut out by their lover's parents at a time like this. She is a wonderful woman."

"I will do my best to do right by Christopher."

"Thanks. I know you will. I better put a sign up on the door now that we will be closed on Saturday for the funeral."

"I'll take care of it. You just work on his flowers."

Dori had insisted on a visitation the day before the funeral. Tyler went to the funeral home two hours prior to the start of the public visitation. He wanted to be alone with Christopher. When he got there, he was amazed at the multitude of floral tributes, many of which had come from his shop. Sophie and the new girl had really outdone themselves. He was especially proud of the spray he did for Dori which rested atop the end of Christopher's casket. Right next to the head of the casket were the red roses from Tyler. Both floral sprays looked good. Christopher would have liked them.

Tyler brought his small CD player and began playing Avro Part's *Spiegel im Spiegel*. "You look really nice, Christopher. Still so handsome. I know this is just the body that your spirit used while here on the earth plane." *Right now I need to look at you and talk to you. I know you can hear me. When I heard that you made your transition, I prayed so hard for your Spirit to go immediately into the Light. I know that's where you are now. And know that I did hear you call out my name.*

The music reminded Tyler of the first time he and Christopher went to the symphony. They featured this piece by Avro Part. *I'd never heard of that composer until that night. I was so mesmerized by the music of the grand piano and the violin and the two dancers who told their story of falling in love. They danced in front of the musicians, moving so gracefully.* Tyler recalled that happier time. Swept away, he couldn't take his eyes off the dancers. And then Christopher, with his eyes still on the musicians and dancers, took Tyler's right hand in his left hand and held it tightly. Returning his gaze back to view Christopher's body, *You showed me such tenderness. You gave me so many lovely moments like that.* The tears started to flow softly down Tyler's cheek. "I'm so sorry it took me such a fucking long time to let myself love you. I'm sorry. I was scared and stupid. But you never gave up on me. You were my knight-in-shining-armor. You loved me unconditionally. Chivalry is not dead. Only somebody who never knew you would say that."

Tyler got the courage to touch Christopher's hands; then he let his fingers graze his cheek. "So cold now. It was your Light that used to radiate warmth and love from this body. Gone now.

Christopher, I would have tried so hard to be the man you wanted and needed. I would have left no stone unturned to make you happy. Please know that. I'm going to shut up now. I just want to sit here with you awhile before your mother and the others get here." Smiling, "I will be listening for you to communicate with me again, whenever you're ready. I love you."

It seemed like the line of people extending their sympathy never ended. Tyler was glad for Dori's sake. She and Christopher knew a lot of people. In addition to herself, Dori had listed Tyler as Christopher's fiancé and best friend, as survivors in the obituary.

Tyler was pleased that Dori had listed the Point Foundation, an organization dedicated to giving college scholarships to lesbian, gay, bisexual, and transgender students as a possibility for those wishing to do something in Christopher's memory. Christopher was very interested in the organization. He had told Tyler about it months ago.

The funeral service would be held at the funeral home's adjoining chapel. A stained glass window with an angel was the focal point facing the pews and additional padded folding chairs that had been set up. Following the service, a luncheon would be held at the country club.

At the service, Dori sat in the front pew with Tyler. Karen, Christopher's ex-wife showed up and was very civil to Dori and gave her a slight hug. She just nodded "sorry" to Tyler and moved along. Where she sat, Tyler had no idea. Behind her were Tyler's friends: Dennis, Michael, George, and Al.

Sophie gave a wonderful eulogy. She spoke from the heart. Tyler remembered that Magda always told them both: "No matter what the occasion, no matter how hard it may seem, just ask that Spirit move through your heart, and you will be fine."

After an opening prayer and meditation, there was a hymn. Then Sophie began speaking. She spoke of looking at today as not just the mourning of a life well-lived, but as a celebration of Christopher. Sophie acknowledged that everyone there had fond memories of Christopher and following the morning's service, they would have the opportunity to gather together and share those stories that made him so loved. Sophie talked of being struck by Christopher's passion for life and especially for doing the right thing, no matter how hard it may be. Authenticity was vital to Christopher's well-being. What was important to Christopher Girrardi? Being a good son to Doris, a good boss, a good friend, and a good companion to Tyler.

Sophie invited everyone to join her in a farewell meditation. "Ever so gently close your eyes. In your mind's eye see a large ball of golden white light. As the sphere of light gets closer to you, it gets bigger until it encompasses you and your surroundings. Within the Light, you now see Christopher as you remember him. He is well and smiling. There is a cord connecting you to him. This is your opportunity to tell Christopher anything you still need to say to him. Listen for what he may say to you. Take a moment to do that." Sophie was silent several minutes. "Now it is time to say good bye. The cord connecting you to Christopher is gone. The ball of Light grows smaller and smaller as it returns into the ethers. Take a deep breath and return to this time and place."

In closing, Sophie shared one of Christopher's favorite quotes from Ralph Waldo Emerson.

"To laugh often and much; to win the respect of intelligent people and the affection of children, to leave the world a better place, to know even one life has breathed easier because you have lived. This is to have succeeded."

For the closing song, Tyler had Sarah MacLachlan's song "Angel" played as the funeral directors wheeled the rose laden casket out to the waiting hearse. The funeral attendant motioned for Dori and Tyler followed by Sophie to follow the casket bearing

Christopher's body out of the sanctuary. Arm in arm, Dori and Tyler had tears running softly down their cheeks.

You are with the Angels now, Christopher. We take great comfort in that knowledge.

CHAPTER TWENTY NINE

Somehow Tyler and Dori got through the funeral and the luncheon which followed. That morning, Tyler had prayed to the Creator, asking that Dori and he be given the strength and stamina to get through the day with grace. Tyler was glad for Dori that so many of her friends and people from Christopher's company showed up to pay their respects. Christopher's company had closed the office early on Friday so the employees could attend Friday's visitation and/or the funeral on Saturday. Tyler didn't know as many people. He was grateful for Sophie's company. Some individuals did come up to him and extend their sympathy, but many didn't. *It's okay,* thought Tyler. He guessed that eventually he would have met many of them had he had a longer time with Christopher.

When he got home, Tyler let Sadie out and collapsed on the sofa. After awhile, he got up to let her back inside. He poured himself a glass of moscato, took one sip, made a face, and poured it down the drain. He returned to the living room and sat back down on the sofa. It was so quiet here in the house. *Turn some music on,* he thought. *No, I just want it to be silent. I want quiet.* Leaning back into the security the sofa offered, staring blankly ahead, and focusing on nothing in particular, Tyler eventually fell into a deep sleep. It was the first sound sleep he had since Christopher's death. He dreamed of being with Christopher. They were riding in the Porsche convertible with the top down on a summer day. Christopher was looking ahead, his eyes on the road. Tyler turned to look at Christopher and smiled. He reached over to touch Christopher's thigh when he woke up abruptly to the clock chiming 8:00 a.m. He was reaching over and touching an accent pillow. "Christopher?"

"Shit. I must have been dreaming." It was Sunday morning. The first Sunday in God-knew-how-long that he wasn't going to be with Christopher. Tyler forced himself to get up and take a shower. He made coffee and breakfast, even though he wasn't really hungry. The scrambled eggs and toast smelled good to him but had no taste. He ate three bites of the eggs and gave the rest to Sadie.

"You used to eat alone all of the time, Tyler. God, I miss him so much!"

Awhile later, he called Dori and got her voice mail. "It's Tyler. I'm just wondering how you are today. Call me if you are so inclined. Hugs to you."

Half aloud, "Get busy, Tyler. You're not going to sit here and feel sorry for yourself." He went into his room and stripped the bed, put clean sheets on, and then did a load of laundry. When he went back to his closet to hang up the shirts, he saw the white linen one with the tags still on it that he had taken from Christopher's closet earlier in the week. "So this is what you were going to wear when you married me, huh Chris? I like it. I would have gotten one like it in my size. Because of your football-player's build, this extra large would look like a night shirt on me." He hung it back up at the end of the rod. Then hanging on a hook, he noticed the blue denim shirt of Christopher's that he had worn while helping

Tyler work around the yard a couple of weeks ago. It wasn't really soiled, so Tyler had never washed it. Christopher had gotten warm, and removed it, and wore only his tee-shirt. Tyler took the denim shirt off the hook and walked over to the bed and sat down. Putting the shirt up to his face, he drank in Christopher's scent, perspiration, and cologne mixture still in the fabric. He inhaled it a second and then a third time. Then the dam let loose, and Tyler, his body gently rocking back and forth, sobbed uncontrolably. Sadie came running in to her master, but Tyler ignored her. Finally, when there were no more tears coming, Tyler wiped his face on his own shirt sleeve.

Holding Christopher's shirt close to his heart, Tyler had an epiphany. *Grow up, Tyler. Life sucks sometimes. You can take care of yourself. You always have. You have the tools within you to be happy. So, be happy. Easier said than done today, isn't it? Deep inside you knew you couldn't have loved Christopher the way you eventually did if you hadn't gone through what you did with Ben. Ben was a teacher of yours. Ben did what he had to do, what he could do. It's a funny thing, life is. Two people go through a narrow gate one at a time. The one that goes first waits for the other person to go through as well and catch up. He waits out of love. Only sometimes the second person never catches up. For awhile, I was ahead of Christopher and then, suddenly, he was ahead of me. Luckily for me he waited for me to catch up. God bless him.*

Sometimes you think that you are so far ahead of everyone else spiritually. Maybe. Probably not. You still have so much to learn. Most importantly here, you have known what **love is.** *Lucky you, Tyler.*

Then Tyler looked upward and outward, "Thank you, God, for letting me know Christopher for as long as I did and for letting him love me. I would have liked to have had another thirty or forty years with him, but I don't blame you for wanting him back sooner. Not angry with you, just so sad and so very disappointed." With that, Tyler put Christopher's shirt on his pillow. He would fall to sleep clutching that shirt for months to come.

CHAPTER THIRTY

The next morning, Monday, Tyler was back at work. Sophie was not surprised. She knew it would be better for Tyler to stay busy.

"I'm glad you're back here."

"Thanks, sweetie. I need to stay busy. Besides, I think I'll stay in the office and work on the books. Is the new girl coming in?"

"Kara. Yes. You can meet her this morning."

When Kara came in, Tyler talked to her following introductions.

"Sophie says you do good work and are good with customers. I appreciate you helping us out last week on such short notice. I would like you to continue with us if you would. I can only promise you 20-25 hours a week right now. More hours, of course, when we are busier."

"That would be fine, Mr. Reynolds. I'm going to school right now, so I couldn't work fulltime."

"Please call me Tyler. What are you studying?"

"Interior design."

"That's great. I'm going to let Sophie tell you what she needs help with this morning. With you here, I have the luxury of focusing on the books without being interrupted. Carry on, ladies."

She seems nice, pleasant, thought Tyler. If Sophie liked her, it should all be okay.

About mid-morning, Tyler's cell phone rang. It was Dori.

"Tyler, honey, it's Dori. Forgive me for not returning your call yesterday. I turned my phone off and didn't talk to anyone. But today's okay. How are you doing?"

"I'm okay, all things considered. I'm back at work. It's good to be busy. How are you, Dori?"

"I'm taking it a day at a time. Sometimes an hour at a time."

"I know exactly how you feel. Just know that you can always call me anytime."

"I'm glad for that, Tyler. You're all the family I have now. I have cousins, but real family, close family, it's just you now."

Changing the topic, Dori went on, "I'm meeting with our attorney at 1:00. Can you meet me there at 2:00 this afternoon so we can begin settling Christopher's estate?"

"Sure, but why do you need me there? Dori, you were Christopher's mother. I don't expect anything." Tyler paused to take a breath, "This is awkward."

"It doesn't have to be. Christopher had a will. I have a pretty good idea about how things were left. Let's get through this together and be done with it. Okay? I need you there, Tyler."

"Okay." She gave Tyler the attorney's address and phone number and hung up.

Tyler sat at his desk, staring at the paperwork in front of him. Sophie popped in, "Would you like coffee? I just made a fresh pot. What's up? You look perplexed."

"That was Christopher's mother. They are reading the will today, and she wants me there. Why do I need to be there? We weren't married. I signed a prenuptial agreement that I drew up and gave to Christopher several weeks ago."

"Since you weren't married, I doubt that the document has any validity. Did Christopher sign the agreement as well?"

"I have no idea."

"Whatever happens will be okay."

"I know.

"Go and see what transpires. You'll be fine."

Tyler showed up at the attorney's office ten minutes early. The receptionist told him to have a seat. "Mr. Weaver is expecting you."

Five minutes later, the door to the inner office opened, and Dori walked out smiling with her attorney close at her heels. "Tyler." As she hugged him, "Anthony, this is Tyler Reynolds. He and Christopher were to be married as you know." Tyler recalled seeing the distinguished looking attorney at the funeral.

The gray-haired lawyer smiled and extended his hand to shake Tyler's. "Mr. Reynolds, finally we meet. Please do come in. Dori, I'll call you later."

"Look, please call me Tyler and, Dori, can't you come in with me?"

"If you want me to, I can. No one is going to bite you, Tyler."

"I would like it if you were with me."

They went into Anthony Weaver's private office and sat across from the desk that the attorney occupied.

Dori explained, "Anthony has been our family's attorney for a long time. He'll explain everything."

Anthony began, "Tyler, You may or may not know that Christopher inherited a lot of money and assets from his father. When he completed college, he went to work for his father's company until his death. Christopher inherited money, but the company also made lots of money while Christopher was CEO and president."

Tyler nodded to the attorney.

"Christopher had everything in a trust and upon his death, left a will explaining how his trust was to be dispersed."

"Okay."

"Christopher left his half of the company and the bulk of his estate to Dori."

"I would expect that."

"Christopher also left you his house, its furnishings, his cars, and a portfolio including cash and investments totaling over two million dollars."

"WHAT? Two million? Dollars?"

"That's just the portofolio. With the house and rest of the assets, I would say it's a little over four million before taxes."

Tyler was stunned, and his face showed it. He knew Christopher was wealthy. However, he had honestly never stopped to calculate.

"Both of you please listen to me. Christopher was always generous to me. At one time, money became an issue with me because I told him I couldn't afford to treat him to the kinds of dates and weekends that he treated me to. Well, we worked through that issue. But on my own, after he asked me to marry him, I drew up a prenuptial agreement, signed it, and gave it to him. It stated that no matter what happened, that if for some reason our marriage should end, I didn't want his money." Tyler's voice started to break.

Regaining his composure, "I don't know what he did with that prenup."

"I have it here," Anthony said, holding up the agreement. I advised him that we should draw something up, but he wouldn't hear of it. It's here, unsigned by him. Since the marriage never took place, it's a moot point. This is what he clearly wanted."

"Tyler," Dori said, "Christopher loved you, or he wouldn't have done this. And if you loved him, you will honor his wishes."

"I know. I know, but I can't live in that huge house, not without him."

"Then sell it. Anthony can help you with that. I know that he left you the contents, but there are some things, some photos and memorabilia that I would like. Perhaps you'd let me have those personal things."

"Certainly. When we're ready, we can go through it together. I'd really like it if you would help me with all of this. Please."

Dori smiled and nodded yes, tears softly starting to fall down her cheeks. Tyler's eyes were brimming as well.

Dori asked, "What else do we need to talk about today?" "That's it. I'll be in touch." Addressing Tyler, "You should create a trust to transfer the assets to. I can help you with that unless you have your own attorney that you would like to have draw it up for you."

"Thanks, but I would feel better if you handled it, Mr. Weaver."

"It's Anthony."

"Anthony. Thank you for your help with all of this. It's overwhelming."

"I will be glad to assist you in any way I can. My secretary will call to schedule an appointment with you within the week. In the meantime, you're free to go through the house and its contents. And I know Dori appreciates it as well."

"She's like the mom I never had."

Tyler hugged Dori. "Call me when you want to go to Christopher's house."

Doris and Tyler hugged again and went their separate ways.

Overcome with emotion, Tyler drove back to his flower shop. When he got there, Sophie was closing up. Kara had already left.

"Tyler? Are you alright?"

"I don't know. I guess so. It appears that Christopher pretty much left me everything."

CHAPTER THIRTY ONE

Time marched on quickly, although there were nights when Tyler thought sleep would never come. He quickly settled into a routine. Every morning he arose by 5:30, meditated, went for a three-mile walk, showered, ate breakfast, and was at the shop getting the day underway there.

Three weeks after the funeral, Tyler and Dori plunged into going through Christopher's house. There was no point in putting off the inevitable. Tyler had also met with his new attorney, Anthony Weaver, and set up a trust for himself, putting his house and business into it as well as his inheritance from Christopher. It all went smoothly. Mr. Weaver was helpful, kind, and understanding. He offered to have Christopher's financial advisor call Tyler if he so desired.

"Sure," said Tyler. "I would appreciate that." Tyler felt overwhelmed at times with all of the legal work involved, but he took comfort in having the men Christopher trusted advise him.

Some days, Dori and Tyler didn't get very far in the process of going through Christopher's house without shedding tears. At first if one started, then the other one joined in. Gradually, it shifted so that if one of them started to cry, the other became his or her shoulder to cry on. "Aren't we just a pair?" Dori would say.

"That we are," Tyler replied.

Dori took most of the pictures. If there was a photo that she wanted and Tyler did as well, she had a copy made for him. There was one of Christopher, when he was about ten, with his dad. He was holding up a big salmon that he had caught in Lake Michigan. He was so proud of his catch that day, and his dad was as well. Tyler had a copy made of that one, Christopher's high school graduation picture, Christopher in his college football uniform, and a recent one of Christopher with his shirt open grilling burgers on a Sunday afternoon. Then there was the formal picture of the two of them together that Christopher had taken when the two had become engaged. They had gotten dressed up that night and went to a Ruth's Chris for dinner to celebrate. Tyler already had one like this. He was pleased that Dori wanted Christopher's.

Even in death, Christopher continued to surprise Tyler. It was a Saturday morning, and Tyler and Dori decided to tackle the guest rooms, thinking that it wouldn't take long. Tyler opened the door to one of the bedrooms, expecting to see the bedroom furniture that had always occupied it. Imagine his shock when it was devoid of that. To one side facing the French doors that opened to a porch-like balcony that overlooked the pool and gardens down below were two wing-back chairs covered in a rich burgundy brocade fabric. The chairs were positioned on either side of the largest amethyst geode that Tyler had ever seen. Including its base to stabilize it, the dark purple gemstone stood almost five feet high. *This amethyst is even larger than the big one we saw at the gem show in Chicago!* On a small oval wooden coffee table in front of the chairs and amethyst, was an envelope with Tyler's name on it. He opened the envelope and removed the card, which was a valentine. In Christopher's handwriting was this note: "My Love, I don't think I should have to wait until next Valentine's Day to give you this. Will this room and its furnishings work for your new meditation room? All My Love, Christopher."

Tyler handed the card to Dori so she could read it. He sat, overwhelmed, in one of the chairs. "Yes, Christopher. It works. Thank you." When Tyler had the huge geode and chairs moved to his house, he used a combination of sage, cedar, and sweetgrass to smudge the items. One could never be sure if any negative vibrations might have attached from the workers who mined the stone or those who transported it. He wasn't about to take any chances having unwanted energies in his home. Magda had taught him well.

Dori said she wasn't interested in any of the furniture. Tyler decided he may as well take some of it. He took the king-size bedroom suite and put it in his room. Tyler moved his set to the guest room and gave the daybed that was in there to Good Will. Tyler also took the brown leather sofa, Chris's favorite recliner, and the dinette set in the breakfast nook. The rest he left for the estate sale. Tyler told Dori that he didn't want to leave Christopher's clothing for the sale. "I'm going to take all of his clothing and donate it to the Men's Shelter." Earlier, Tyler had taken all of the non-perishable food items and gave them to a local food pantry. Tyler had decided, too, that with the money from the estate sale as well as the sale of the house, he would set up a scholarship fund in Christopher's memory as part of the local community foundation. The advisors there would help him determine the size of the college scholarships to be given annually. Tyler decided they would go to students in the performing arts. He would also see that the local symphony got money in Christopher's memory as well. A peaceful feeling descended on Tyler when he had decided to do this. As far as the money and portfolio that Christopher had left him, they could remain in the trust indefinitely. *I don't need to touch that*, thought Tyler.

One Sunday morning Tyler was in his backyard drinking coffee, watching Sadie chase a butterfly. Staring at the rear portion of the yard, he thought, *I'm going to make a rose garden for Christopher.* He walked around the area, pacing it off as to the size it could be. To Sadie he said, "I'm going to get some patio tile and put a bench in one corner. There can be a fire pit in the center. A fire would be good on those chilly nights when we want to be out here looking at the stars. We'll put rose bushes in that corner spot and accent it the perimeter with hostas."

Tyler got to work that day. He went to a landscaping supply store and ordered the patio tile to be delivered that week. The next stop was a nursery where he purchased four rose bushes, each a different color. One was lavender blue. The others were a coral-orange, a deep golden yellow, and a vibrant red. He picked out several varieties of hosta which boasted an assortment of shades of green leaves. Some plants had a lighter green or yellow as a border of each leaf. Others were solid, broad leaves of forest green. The garden would be spectacular when in full bloom.

He spent his evenings and weekends creating the new garden. When he completed it, he stepped back to evaluate it. *It needs a three-tier water fountain centered between the rose bushes,* he thought. Once he obtained the fountain and secured it in place, he invited Sophie over to see his recent endeavor.

"This is lovely, Tyler. What a beautiful space you have created. Christopher would have loved it."

"I thought I would have heard something more from him by now," Tyler lamented to Sophie when she came to see his new garden. "I try so hard to be open for something, some sign, anything. I know that he is okay. When I learned about the accident, I asked that he go into the Light immediately. I pray for him every day that he is fine and adjusted to life as it is on the other side. It must have been a terrible jolt to the system to be taken out of the physical body so suddenly like he was."

Sophie smiled, "Remember it was awhile before we heard from Magda, and she was so evolved and knew that she was going to transition when she did. So be patient with Christopher. When you both are ready, you will hear from him.

"I know. I miss him so much."

"Maybe your sadness is preventing him from reaching you. It's just a thought."

"Sometimes I can't help being so sad. I try not to but there are times I still cry myself to sleep."

"That's okay. But the next time you're sad and missing Christopher, what if you try saying, 'Okay, Christopher, I admit it. I'm missing you like crazy. I'm incredibly sad you're not here with me. Nonetheless, I am happy for you. Joyful that you are Home with your Star People, and are once again in the bliss of the White Light. Try it. What do you have to lose? As with any affirmation, keep saying it until you believe it."

"Okay, I will."

Sophie became a blur as Tyler repeated his new mantra. "I'm happy for you, Christopher. I'm happy for you. I'm happy for you, so very happy." Tyler opened his eyes. It was dark save for the stars and the new moon's light. He heard the gentle lapping of the waves against the shore. Where was he? Had he fallen asleep and been dreaming? "Hmmmm, I'm still at the lake. I must have zoned out. The cool night air didn't wake me." Glancing at his watch, "Oh my God, it's 4:00 in the morning. I have been here all night!"

Tyler stared up at the clear sky. The New Moon was beautiful and graceful in her own right. He stared at the stars. A twinkling star far away in the sky caught Tyler's attention. He stared at it, smiling. "That star is so beautiful. I believe it's twinkling brightly just for me." As he focused on this particular star, much to Tyler's amazement, the star slowly seemed to be getting closer. *Oh my!* The star moved closer and closer as Tyler became mesmerized by its approach. "Wait a minute. Wait just a damn minute! Christopher always said he was from the Star People and that the stars were his home." Was this star bringing him a message from Christopher? "Do you have a message from him for me?" The star now was ten feet away. It's white, dazzling light was so bright. Tyler raised his hand over his eyes to shield them. The starlight morphed into a vertical shaft of pure white light. In a whisper, "Holy shit!"

Tyler's eyes adjusted to the bright light. As he stared at its brilliance, its shape shifted into the very image of Christopher. Crying, "Oh my God, Christopher, it's really you! I must be dreaming."

"You're not dreaming Tyler. It's me."

"Christopher!"

"Relax, Tyler. We don't have much time."

"Where do I start? I love you so much!"

"I know you do. It's your love that raised your vibration enough that allowed me to be here."

To accurately describe Christopher's aura was not easy. It was a shimmering silver and white light. Tyler wanted to touch him so badly but out of intrinsic respect for the moment, he did not.

"We don't have much time. Thank you for all of your prayers and the love you've sent to me. They helped me immensely to adjust to life on the other side of the veil."

"I didn't love you enough. I'm sorry."

"Stop beating yourself up. Our relationship unfolded as it was supposed to. I knew that you loved me long before you had the courage to say so."

"You never gave up on me. Thank you."

Christopher smiled, "Sometimes you can't help who you love."

Nodding and smiling back at Christopher, "A wise man told me that once." Taking a deep breath Tyler asked, "What was it like when you crossed over? Did you feel pain from the accident?"

"No, none at all. My spirit, my soul, immediately left my physical body and hovered above the car until help came. I thought then 'I must be dead.' I remember being drawn to this incredibly beautiful light. I could hear music, like a symphony playing. It was far more beautiful than we ever imagined when you and I used to talk about it. Then I heard an angel's voice: 'Your work on the earth plane is finished. You can come home now.' I looked down at my mangled body, and I knew how you and Mother would react. "But I have people who love me there. And the voice said: 'You can return if you choose. This is your second window of opportunity to leave the earth plane. You must choose.' I hesitated because I loved you so much. And then the voice said: 'There is no right or wrong decision, but choose now.' So I went into the Light."

"Wait a minute. You had a choice?! Why would you not come back to me, especially if you had the chance?"

"Tyler, Tyler," Christopher was smiling and shaking his head. "Everything is NOT always about YOU. This was my journey. My contract was to teach you to trust, to love again. It wasn't easy but, I fulfilled my contract." Christopher paused, "You will have the opportunity to love again on the earth plane if you so choose."

Tyler listened intently. "I understand what you're saying, but I'm not so sure I could ever do that again. I know how much you love me, or you wouldn't have come here like this."

"My dad and your friend Magda were there to assist me in going into the Light. It was so good to see Dad again."

"That's wonderful! Your father and you saw Magda?!"

"Yes, she's fine. She loves you very much."

"What do you do over there, Christopher?"

"I help souls who were taken out suddenly as I was, adjust to the Light. It's rewarding. Tyler, there is such love here. The words you have on the earth plane cannot adequately describe the colors and the emotions here."

"I want so much to touch you, to hold you again. Please let me touch you, Christopher."

"Close your eyes and you can feel me. That's all that's allowed."

Tyler did as requested. It was so real. When Christopher continued speaking he opened them to once more see this miraculous vision.

"You have lots of work to do yet, Tyler, before it's time for you to make your transition. But when you're ready, I will be there for you to help you cross over. Know I was honored to be your fiancé and lover."

Tyler blinked his eyes rapidly. The image of Christopher was starting to dim.

"You're starting to fade. Don't go, not yet. I love you so much."

"Be strong, Tyler. You have it in you."

As Christopher continued to gradually fade, "It was so much easier to be strong when you were here."

"You helped me believe in myself, and I believed in you. That hasn't changed. I'm only a thought away. Be strong for yourself and in so doing, you will be strong for everyone."

"I'll try."

"I wish that you could always see how astonishing the Light is that you radiate. Even when you feel alone or in the dark, you radiate a magnificent Light. It's what drew me to you."

"Thank you, Christopher, for everything. You taught me so much. I will try my damnedest to walk the Red Road. Not just because it's the right thing to do, but to honor you." The tears flowed freely down Tyler's cheeks. "You're fading. Please don't leave. Please stay with me."

In a loud echoing voice from the heavens, Tyler heard Christopher's departing words, "There is great love for you here." And just like that, Christopher was gone.

CHAPTER THIRTY TWO

Tyler remained seated on the log surrounded by beach grass. He wiped the tears from his cheeks and smiled. He started humming George Winston's song "Angel." The Angels always brought Tyler comfort. Tyler was grateful for his belief system. "Thank you God. Thank you, Universe. THANK YOU, CHRISTOPHER. I am so blessed."

Reveling in what had just happened, Tyler didn't want to move. Other than Sophie, who would believe him as to this awesome experience? The sun was coming up. He glanced at the sky and noticed Mother Moon was disappearing until the next evening. But the star, Christopher's star, was still twinkling at him in the distance.

Tyler stood and stretched before starting the walk back to the parking lot. It was then that he noticed a male figure approaching him. He looked around, and there was no one else there on the beach. It wasn't unusual for early-morning joggers to be here, but this man was walking directly toward him.

"Tyler? Tyler?"

It was Ben. Tyler couldn't remember when he had last seen him. As Ben approached, Tyler noticed his unkempt appearance. He needed a haircut, hadn't shaved in several days, rumpled clothes. He looked like a hot mess. This was so unlike him. "I need to talk to you. I stopped by your house several times last night and then again early this morning, and you still weren't home. I remembered you said once that you came here to meditate. So I took the chance that I'd find you here." Ben paused and looked deeply into Tyler's eyes. "Have you been crying? Are you okay?"

"I'm fine. Thank you for asking. What is so important that after all this time you would come looking for me?"

"I need to talk. I need a friend. You're the only one I can turn to."

"That sounds a bit dramatic. No one in your congregation you can talk to?"

"No. Haven't you heard? There isn't much of a congregation left. The church closed its doors last week."

"Thought perhaps it was just a rumor."

"Not a rumor. The truth."

"The energies are changing around us. Churches will close. The Universe doesn't like hypocrisy. People are standing up for and demanding truth, honesty, and integrity."

"I know that now."

"Ben, when I left your church, people called or emailed and said, "We'll still stay in touch. We'll still be friends. While I was an active member there whenever someone lost someone close to him, I sent a card. I sent flowers. I went to visitations because that is what a friend does. When Christopher died, I didn't hear from one fucking person, not one, from your beloved congregation."

Saying nothing, Ben stared down at the sand. Finally, he spoke. "I'm sorry, Tyler, for hurting you."

"There was a time in my life when I longed for you to say those words. Now that you have, it's rather anti-climactic. Time and forgiveness heals all things. What's up with you? You look distraught."

"My wife left me."

"Oh? I thought that you two were very happy together."

"I thought I could make it work. It got so that when we did have sex, which was happening less and less...." Ben's voice trailed off.

"And?"

Ben glanced at Tyler as he continued, "I couldn't perform unless I was fantasizing about being with men."

"Ah, the forbidden raised its ugly head. What happened? Did you confess your fantasies to her?"

"No, worse, she caught me in bed with another man."

"Imagine that! You were in bed with another man? What strange behavior for an avowed heterosexual like yourself."

"Look, I know things didn't end nicely with us."

"I loved you, Ben. I loved you terribly. I believed in you. I thought that you believed in me. When you left me the way you did, my heart was ripped out. I blamed myself for awhile. I tried too hard. I didn't try hard enough. We were soul-mates, but you couldn't buy into that. Why couldn't you?"

Ben remained silent.

"My contract with you was to help you be authentic, to embrace your authentic self. You rejected that. It must have taken an incredible amount of energy to maintain that façade. For the longest time, I thought you would come around and be honest with yourself about who you were."

"I couldn't be open like you are, Tyler."

"For the longest time I really hated you. Unfortunately for me, that hatred was consuming me. It didn't change a thing. Then one day, I had this huge epiphany. You were not in the same relationship with me that I was in with you. It was that simple. I forgave you, and I forgave myself for loving you." Tyler was surprised at how calmly and rationally he could share this revelation with

Ben. "And so I mean this with all sincerity. You loved me enough to teach me a valuable lesson. I thank you."

Stunned, Ben mumbled, "I didn't expect to hear that."

"You sought me out to talk. How can I help you, Ben?"

"I'm at rock-bottom. I have nothing. No marriage, no partner, no job, no friends. I put everything into my ministry. The attendance dwindled, along with the contributions. I'm destitute. I don't know where to turn."

"Ben, the Phoenix comes for all of us at one time or another, in one way or another. Now it has come for you. It's a wake-up call. You have been given the opportunity to rise from the ashes and be your authentic self now."

"How do I do that?"

"One step at a time. Now that you know what doesn't work anymore, you can focus on what does. Trust me, one day you will look back on all of this and say Thank You to the Divine for giving you a good swift kick."

"How do you know what to do?"

"I listen to my heart for starters. I meditate."

"That really works?"

"It does for me. Try it. It makes difficult things easier. I had love taken from me twice: once with you, then with Christopher. That was really hard. Still is. But I've grown. You can, too, from this. It's not the end of the world. It just seems like it."

"Tyler, do you think that we can be friends again?"

Shaking his head, "I don't know. I'm not so sure we ever were friends."

Ben said nothing. Then at a loss, "I'm sorry about Christopher."

"Me, too. I can feel his love around me, and it's enough."

Awkwardly Ben blurted out, "Where do we go from here?"

"There is no 'we.' You should start by going home, taking a long hot shower, and shaving. Individually, we will move forward."

"I hope so. What about you? Now that Christopher is gone."

Tyler blurted out, "I'm going to Italy."

Tyler smiled to himself. He made that decision as the words came out of his mouth. Christopher had said he would take him there. Sophie could manage the flower shop. He would make her his full business partner. *I'll tell her this morning, then make travel arrangements.*

"Are you going all the way to Italy by yourself?"

"It might appear to others that I'm traveling alone, but the reality is that I'm never alone. Not anymore." Clutching his heart, "Everything I've ever needed has been right here inside all along. I know that now."

Ben looked at Tyler trying to comprehend.

"There was a new moon last night. The sun is rising today. That means there is always hope. There is the opportunity for new beginnings, Ben."

Tyler looked skyward, and Ben followed his stare.

It was Ben who noticed the lone star still remaining in the morning sky, twinkling brightly. "Look at that star. It's the only one left in the sky."

"That's my lucky star," Tyler responded. Tyler knew in his heart of hearts that his Star Being, Christopher, was shining down on him. That bright Light would illuminate his journey for years to come. Because of it, Tyler knew he would always have hope and love. Most importantly, he knew there was great love for him.

LOVE IS INVINCIBLE.

And so it is.

ACKNOWLEGEMENTS

Without the love, support and assistance from the following this book would never have happened. Thank you Camille Albrecht, Jim Canter, Eddie Conner, Arlene Hecksel, Denise Iwaniw, Gary Samples, Laureen Samples, and Cliff Young.

Made in the USA
Middletown, DE
23 June 2015